GUNSHIPS: The Killing Zone

There were many dark and dreadful stories in the hell that was Vietnam . . .

It is a land where every tree and bush can kill, where the most lethal technology of war is allied with man's basest instincts, where a soldier's bloodlust can throttle his better self like a jungle creeper. And sometimes a man had less to fear from the enemy than from his own side.

John Hardin, Colonel in the US Special Forces, knows a lot about the dirty side of war—and his knowledge could be disastrous for his military superiors. He has to be silenced. And a hand-picked squad of mongrels and misfits are destined to die with him in the rotting swamps and festering paddy fields that make up 'The Killing Zone'.

A blistering story of men caught in a war where glory was a dirty word and every man a loser!

GUNSHIPS
The Killing Zone

Jack Hamilton Teed

CHIVERS PRESS
BATH

First published in Great Britain 1981 by Star Books,
the Paperback Division of W.H. Allen & Co Ltd

First hardback edition 1983 by Chivers Press
by arrangement with W. H. Allen & Co Ltd

0 85997 516 9

British Library Cataloguing in Publication Data

Teed, Jack Hamilton
Gunships: the killing zone.
I. Title
813'.54[F]   PS3570.E/

ISBN 0–85997 516–9

To

DAVE HUNT

—A great editor—
who first dragged me
kicking and screaming
into the war business

PROLOGUE

A fly buzzed past Hardin's nose at an angle and headed for the window. It was blue-green and fat and noisy. It was also—and probably, Hardin supposed, this was the same for flies the world over—entirely devoid of intelligence.

There was no glass in the window, only a copper-hued metal grille. The holes in the grille were wide enough for the insect to fly through with ease, but each time it tried this it stubbornly headed straight for one of the bars, baulked when it came to within an inch or so of the obstruction, zoomed up and over in a stunt-roll, then tried again. It kept on doing this. A fat and noisy and stupid fly. Either that or its radar was on the fritz. If flies had radar. Hardin didn't know.

The window grille was ornate in design, a relic, like the peeling wooden shutters outside, now open to let the hot white sunlight into the room, of French colonial rule. The hotel itself, standing in a quiet Saigon side-street near the cathedral, was narrow-fronted but long and rambling behind. It dated from before the First World War; possibly from before 1900. Certainly from an era of gracious living.

The rooms were large and spacious, even the bathrooms; the front hall was as high as the nave in a medium-sized church, with a central staircase that drifted upwards in a wide sweeping curve. There was a long bar leading off from the reception area that still retained many of its original Art Nouveau fittings; lamp-brackets in the walls made of opaque glass and shaped like drooping lilies, huge curved mirrors, absurd floral clusters in tarnished silver hanging over the tall windows that looked out onto the street. The sort of place where the old-timers used to drink their Pernod straight; no water, no ice.

Hardin tried to visualise these old-timers, but the pictures in his mind were vague, would not come alive. Planters and administrators, for the most part; maybe the odd French Army officer, too, though as a breed they preferred other, more clannish watering-places elsewhere in town. No one famous, though. A minor French poet had committed suicide here (Room 23, on the second floor) sometime during the 1920's, but that was all. Cut his wrists open and bled to death in his bath. But he was a very minor French poet; Hardin couldn't even remember his name.

If he'd done it during the 1890's, that would have been different, of course (always assuming the hotel had existed in the 1890s). Bleeding to death in the bath was a kind of a decadent thing to do; it went with drooping lilies and wide curving staircases and hands with long shapely fingers fashioned out of ivory and crazy chandeliers with 250 crystal tears hanging from them. It would have sanctified him, somehow, however lousy his poetry was; made him a part of the mythology of the times.

But no. The dumb fucker had to do it during the 1920s, when the hotel dance-band was probably thumping out a tango downstairs, and Noël Coward was writing comic songs in the Continental a couple of blocks away.

Craning his neck slightly, as he peered out through the window grille, Hardin could just see the end of the road, where it opened out into Tu Do Street. The dust raised by the explosion had long since settled, and the body been cleared away, though no one had bothered to mop up the long smears of blood that darkened the corner pavement, or dust them with chloride of lime. The rain, when it came, would wash those away.

A couple of Arvin MPs with slung M-16s were lounging against a shop window, smoking. As Hardin watched, an old woman in black tunic and trousers came past, stopped, stared at where the blood was. One of the MPs yelled at her and unslung his rifle, poking the barrel at her. The old woman went off quickly, and the MP threw his cigarette after her, still shouting.

Another dumb fucker, thought Hardin; then back-pedalled in his mind. He wasn't quite sure whether he meant the old woman or the Arvin MP. And then he realised that the real dumb fucker—much dumber than the minor French poet whose name he couldn't remember, or even, come to think of it, the fat noisy fly still trying to escape past him through the grille and still failing—was the young guy he'd last seen lying spreadeagled across the corner sidewalk, with most of the contents of his stomach

2

spread around him.

'Jesus Christ, Hardin. I didn't ask you up here to admire the view.'

'I realise that, General. I was just mulling over what you've been saying.'

Hardin never called General Dempsey 'sir'. But never. There were many people, spread out over the entire length and breadth of South Vietnam, that Hardin didn't like, and there were a few he hated. Dempsey was the only man he actively despised.

'There's nothing to mull over, Hardin. You just say yes, and get your ass out of here and up-country.'

Hardin breathed air out of his lungs in a short, irritated sigh. It looked as though he was going to have to blow his hand—a hand he'd built up with great care over a period of nine months or more. A hand he'd built up for just such an emergency as this, actually, but that wasn't the point. It was never a smart move to reveal all your cards at once, and that was what it seemed he was going to have to do any minute now.

'For Chrissake, Hardin. What exactly the fuck is it out there that you can't take your eyes off it?'

The two MPs had wandered off round the corner, and the end of the street was empty now. The only sign of movement was traffic in Tu Do: jeeps, old Citroëns, tricycle taxis, red Hondas with laughing girls on them.

'I was just thinking about the explosion, General.'

'So the explosion. So what the hell.'

'You didn't hear it?'

'Sure I heard it. Shook the whole fucking hotel. Christ on a crutch, Hardin, we get explosions two a day in this fucking ville. Luke the Gook's tossing grenades these days like it's confetti.'

Hardin shook his head, still peering through the window.

'It was a *plastique*. Destroyed a couple of shops up Tu Do. I was walking on the other side of the road, just behind a bunch of Arvin MPs, when it happened. Whoompf. Dust everywhere, kids screaming, women yelling, glass all over the road. Usual thing. But a guy suddenly appeared from nowhere, running like he was in the 100-metres dash, and

3

two of the Arvins took him out. Just blew him away.'

'I know what you're going to say,' interrupted Dempsey. 'You're going to say: the only trouble was, the guy they wasted was the Mayor of Saigon.'

'No,' said Hardin. 'The only trouble was, the guy was a Marine Sergeant.'

Behind him Dempsey laughed, a hoarse coughing sound.

'Jesus, that's rich. That'll tie the Admin up for months. It'll take a truckload of paperwork to sort that out.'

Hardin fished a cigarette out of the crumpled pack in his breast pocket and Zippoed it. He blew smoke out of his mouth in a long blue-grey plume and watched it destroy itself against the window grille.

'The jerk must've arrived in Nam yesterday,' Dempsey went on. 'Jesus. I mean, the first thing you learn in this town is, if you hear a bang you stay put. Even if it's only a firecracker. You don't run towards it, and you don't run away from it. Especially you don't run away from it. Preferably you stay right where you are for about fifteen fucking minutes, because if you move you're dead. You're fucking dead. I figured that out within a half hour of landing here, Hardin. It's called survival.'

Hardin turned from the window and walked across the room to where a chest of drawers stood against the wall. On top was a heavy glass ashtray, and he carefully deposited his ash in the centre of it.

'This is a kind of a strange briefing, General,' he said.

'Hell, Hardin, you've been in Special Forces long enough to know that some briefings have to suit the, uh ... exigencies of the situation.'

He looked, sitting in the armchair in the corner of the room nearest the door, with the light from the bent-arm lamp on the table next to him only illuminating his face from the chin down, like some grossly evil spider two seconds before it springs out for the kill.

He was in shirt-sleeves, and his thick hairy arms lay along the arm-rests of the chair, spatulate fingers curled over the ends. His belt was loose and the button-clip at the top of his pants undone, the bulk of his stomach sagging downwards in folds. His legs were side apart, the calves

4

resting against the sides of the chair.

To a casual observer he would have looked relaxed, but Hardin knew otherwise; he'd sensed the tension when he'd first entered the room. Dempsey was expecting trouble from him, and that meant there was something screwy about the mission. Apart from anything else, why was Dempsey briefing him here, instead of back at Base?

'The way I see it, General, I'm to head a three-man team up into southern Laos and track the 10th and 14th North Vietnamese Rangers, who are supposed to be working the area. They might move across the line into South Vietnam, on the other hand they might not. All we do is watch them and keep HQ informed of their movements; no overt action. This could take us a couple of weeks. There'll be a cache prepared for us in a village called Mek Lonh, but there'll be no field linkups with any other units, either Special Forces or friendly Laotians.' He glanced at Dempsey. 'Right?'

Dempsey nodded, dipping his head so that the rest of his face came down into the lamp-light. His black hair was sparse, slicked back in streaks over mottled skin. His eyebrows were thick tufts of black hair that almost hid eyes that were as small as a pig's. His nose was fleshy, a parrot's beak in profile.

'That's about the shape of it.'

Hardin took a pull at his cigarette, then stubbed it out in the ashtray.

'To be frank, General, it doesn't make a hell of a lot of sense. It's a piss-bucket intelligence job. Any warrant-officer could take it out. Why me?'

Dempsey shifted slightly in his chair.

'You're good, Hardin,' he said carefully.

'That's how I got to be a Colonel at 32, General.'

'Well, sure.'

'So why waste me on something like this, General?'

'Yeah. Well. There are certain other factors to be taken into consideration.'

'Like what?'

Hardin was beginning to feel real anger building up inside him. All of this was simply absurd. Dempsey clearly wanted something off him very badly, but he'd blown his whole approach. The entire build-up—the hotel, the secret interview, this pussyfooting around whatever it was he wanted done—was an insanely botched job. Dempsey, for some reason, was desperate.

'This is an important mission, Hardin. Very important. We need to know exactly what these particular NVA groups are doing. We, uh ... very much need to know. Things are heating up in the north. We can do without another Tet, especially right now with all the shit that's flying back home. Jesus. Fucking students mobbing the Goddamn White House, and don't tell me the fucking Reds aren't behind that. Right. We've got to firm up this whole thing or the cat'll really be out of the valise. Let me tell you, Hardin, that we have solid intelligence that Laos is starting to think about kissing Charlie's ass. They're talking about letting supplies go through on the Ho Chi Minh Trail, just so long as the NVA haul ass out of Laos itself. A reciprocal arrangement; titty for tatty. Can you believe that? I'm telling you, Hardin, we have to pull the strings tight on this one fast or the whole fucking barrel'll go straight down the tube.'

Hardin had heard about the Laotian arrangement, but couldn't figure out for the moment why Dempsey should be so worked up about it. It might only be propaganda, or even a rumour. And even if it were true and the Laotians actually meant what they said, that did not necessarily mean they would stick to it. In two months time—or two weeks, or even two days—things might have altered considerably. There was nothing solid about the situation in South East Asia. Well, apart from the Americans pulling back out of the western border area in between the fourteenth and fifteenth parallels. That was solid. Or at least, as solid as any politically-motivated goodwill gesture—to be produced out of the hat at the renewed Paris truce negotiations in a month or so's time—could be said to be solid.

Dempsey pulled a handkerchief out of his pocket and dabbed at his brow. He was breathing heavily, and shaking his head and muttering 'Jesus' every two or three seconds. He thumped the chair-arm with his right fist.

'Okay. So that's how it is, and that's what we want you to

do. Check out that whole border zone and keep tight up Charlie's ass. I mean, all the way. You're on your own up there. Don't need me to tell you that. Like I said, no linkups with friendlys in the field. Solo strat. You've never worked that area before, but Mek Lonh is a solid ville, heavy for us. No problems there at all. They hate the EnVees worse than poison, but naturally they have to be circumspect. Still. You'll in fact, apart from retrieving the cache, will be carrying out one drop in the area, nothing big deal, in the ville itself, which is kind of important.'

Hardin said, 'What about this drop?'

He knew he had his finger on what was bothering Dempsey now. All he had to do was press. Press hard. Not let go for a moment.

Dempsey lifted a hand; made a vague gesture.

'Like I said, nothing big deal. A job, like anything else in this crappy war. Some drop or other. To oblige the spooks. You get the drift?'

'I'm beginning to,' said Hardin. 'Some sort of package, I guess. Not too heavy?'

'Sure, some kind of packet. Light-weight. Jesus. Hardin, I'm not asking you to haul a carton of canned beans through bandit country. You could slip it in your pouch.'

'Could,' said Hardin, 'but won't, General.'

For a General, Dempsey was unusual in that, as far as Hardin could tell, he had no combat rating at all. Basically he was a desk man from way back; Korea, in fact. But that hadn't stopped him climbing. He was tricky, as twisty as a corkscrew, and he was vindictive, and those were two very good reasons why he'd kept his position in Vietnam when more capable but less malicious men had fallen by the wayside. His status in Special Forces was only vaguely defined, but he had strong connections with the CIA, and he carried clout, there was no doubt about that. There were other hookups Hardin had discovered, more tenuous than those with the CIA, yet infinitely more dangerous; Dempsey swam in very dark and murky waters indeed.

It now looked like he was in some really deep shit—up to his eyebrows; maybe even up to the roots of his hair—and going down fast. He was desperate for someone to pull him out. That was the only explanation for this clumsy attempt to pull Hardin in on a job that clearly had very little official sanction.

Now, Dempsey said slowly, almost uncomprehendingly, 'What did you say?'

'I won't do it, General.'

'What the hell does that mean?'

'It means I think this sucks. I've done some pretty strange things over the past five, six years, some pretty bizarre and vicious jobs, but I'm not pulling your chestnuts out of the fire. Get some other sucker, or do it yourself. Either way, include me out.'

Dempsey came out of his chair like an unleashed Jack-in-the-Box.

'You motherfucking son of a bitch, Hardin. You'll do as I say, hear? You'll take my orders.'

'Put them through the proper channels, General. And even, then, forget it.'

'You'll take my orders and you'll get the hell up-country and do what I say.'

'No way, General.'

'Jesus Christ on a fucking crutch, you little fuckhead, you'll do what I say or I'll bust you.'

'Go screw yourself, General.'

'I'll bust you into the dirtiest fucking brig in Nam,' screamed Dempsey. 'I'll bust you right across the fucking Pacific and back again.'

'Pull your pants up, General. You present a ludicrous spectacle.'

Dempsey was in a half-crouch, his face red and blotched, his teeth bared, his right arm jabbed out, one quivering forefinger pointing at Hardin. His loosened pants had slipped halfway down his thighs.

He yanked them up and tugged his belt tight, then sank back into the chair, breathing harshly. Droplets of sweat ran down his forehead and between his brows. He wiped them away with his handkerchief.

'All this is really very fucking irrational, Hardin. I mean, I got no wish to bust your ass, but you're really being very unreasonable. Jesus, man, I've never come across an attitude like yours before. You'll get me to thinking you've gone *dinky dau* unless you tighten up damn fast.'

8

Hardin shrugged. As far as he was concerned the crisis had passed. From now on it was hey diddle diddle, straight down the middle. Dempsey was going to keep pushing him, and he was going to have to heave right back, and Dempsey, though he didn't know it, was going to take a backwards tumble on his fat ass, from which he would not be able to get up again for a long time. If he ever got up at all.

'I mean, let's play around with this situation, Colonel. Getting right down to the nitty-gritty, you just disobeyed an order ... from a *general*!' Dempsey's voice, normally something of a harsh croak, slid up an octave or so. 'Well, Jesus, Hardin, in some folks' books, that'd come right down to outright fucking *treason*!'

Hardin pinched the bridge of his nose and wondered how quickly he could get this farce over, and head out into the comparative reality of the Saigon street. He suddenly felt very tired, and hot, and bored.

'Getting right down to the nitty-gritty, as you say, General, here's the scenario the way I figure it. You, for some reason I'm not even all that interested in, are in deep shit. To get out of this deep shit, you need to get something to a point that is 250, 300 miles away, and this has to be done by a certain date. It just so happens there is EnVee movement that needs watching not all that far away from where this something has to be in a week or so. Okay,' Hardin lit a cigarette as he talked, quietly and firmly, tolerating no interruption, letting his eyes follow the drift of smoke as it died out across the room, 'so you need someone to make the drop. *But*—and this is the kicker— you need someone a damn sight more reliable than the bad-ass crudheads who normally fix for you in situations like this. This something you have to deliver up-country is as nervous as sweaty nitroglycerine in the wrong hands, and you can't take the chance of letting some guy who just might turn out to be even more crooked than you are coming within 250, 300 *inches* of it. You need someone you can trust.'

He looked at Dempsey, and Dempsey stared back, the knuckles of his hands white where he gripped the arms of the chair. Hardin grinned.

'I've got to say, General,' he said, 'that it's an honour to be so categorised. I mean, to be thought of as a man of probity in this badman's war is—well, I feel kind of distinguished. Even so, General, I have to say that you're going to have to find another patsy, or bite on the bullet and take what's coming to you. And whatever it is, it couldn't happen to a sweeter guy.'

Dempsey had gone back into his spider-crouch, but lower in the chair. The light now shone on the top of his head, creating shadows under his eyebrows, nose and chin. He looked like a malevolent goblin.

'You'll do this, Hardin,' he whispered, with complete assurance in his voice. 'You have no choice in the matter.'

Hardin shook his head; laughed.

'Wise up, General. You're in a bad position. You're outflanked. You've got nothing on me that you can use, or you'd have spat it out by now. You must be in one hell of a fix, or you'd have thought this out a whole lot more carefully. Face it, if I'd been called in and briefed at Base with two or three other guys, told to head up north, shadow Charlie, and drop a package, sure, I might've thought it was kind of crazy, me being a Colonel and all, and this being a two-bit job, but then this is a crazy war, and we all have to do crazy things from time to time.'

Hardin turned and flicked his cigarette across the room. It went straight through one of the gaps in the window grille and disappeared from sight.

'But, frankly, you blew it.'

For the first time Dempsey smiled, a thin crinkle of humourless mirth that flickered briefly across his face.

'I'm gonna break your balls for this, Hardin.'

Hardin shook his head.

'No, General. With great disrespect, you are not going to break my balls. You are not even going to break the nail on my little finger. I'll admit I'm not exactly Mr Kleen, and I have ribbons to prove it, but you have to hand it to me: I am a fucking honourable man. As compared with, let's say, you.'

Dempsey made no movement of his body; only his eyes shifted slightly, maybe refocused.

'Keep digging your own grave, Colonel,' he said, from

deep down in his throat.

'Sure. Why beat about the old banana tree, General? Why don't I give you a few fer-instances. Like, fer instance, you own this hotel; strange deeds are done here. Like, fer instance, you own three, maybe four boom-boom houses in this fair city; even stranger deeds are done there.'

'All this is chicken-shit, Hardin, gnat's piss. Mere crapola.'

Hardin nodded.

'Affirm on that. But can the same be said of your connections with certain Vietnamese politicians who have rather more unlikely, not to say bizarre, connections of their own? Connections, I might add, and not that I need to, that would not look too damn healthy under a two-cent plastic magnifying glass you could buy off a concession stall in Coney Island, let alone a Courts Martial microscope.'

As he was speaking, Hardin was moving across the room, stepping over foot-stools and gaily-patterned cushions and small spindly-legged tables with bowls of flowers on them. He moved swiftly, sure-footed amidst the domestic debris. He had a tight smile on his face.

He reached the table next to Dempsey and placed both hands on it, leaning down towards the man, and speaking in a low, confidential tone.

'And here's the big one, General. Here's the 70,000 pound bomb-load all at once. I know you're trying to squeeze the lid down tight on a civilian massacre instigated and controlled by you that'll make My Lai look like an end of semester pantie raid.'

Although he was looking straight down into Dempsey's eyes, it seemed to Hardin that there was no life at all in them. Even the lids didn't flutter. They were as dead as pebbles lying on the surface of the moon.

Suddenly, Dempsey said 'I'll . . .' in a surprisingly strong voice, but he didn't say anything more.

'Cat got your tongue, General?'

Hardin wondered if he ought to quit now, and then decided, the hell with it; he might as well push it to the limit.

'Like you say, there's a lot of shit flying back home. Not

11

to put too fine a point on it, the conduct of the war is viewed with some suspicion by a hell of a lot of people. A lot of very alarming and shitty things have been done, you might say, in the name of America.'

Hardin was beginning to feel good now, as though he'd been hitting some prime Laotian Red. His nerve-ends were almost starting to tingle.

'You know and I know what the great American public don't know: that My Lai is just the tip of the shit-pile. In fact, the great American public don't really want to know, but they're getting their noses rubbed in it whether they want it or not. But the howls of indignation over My Lai will be as worm farts, General, to the shrieks of revulsion over Tun Phouc, should that ever hit the headlines. Upwards of 900 dead, I believe? Man, it'll gross 'em out!'

Outside in the street someone changed gear inexpertly. Hardin sauntered across to the window and stood in the hot sunlight, looking out. There was nothing much to see. The fat fly zoomed down from the ceiling and renewed its attack on the window, with the same amount of success as before.

'Upwards of 900,' Hardin repeated thoughtfully. 'That's a real bummer, General.' His fingers felt for his cigarettes, and then decided against it. He was smoking too much anyway. 'Smart of you to split the unit up, but not smart enough. Once these Goddamn newspapermen get their teeth into something tasty, they never stop. They'll go on chewing till they've extracted every last milligram of blood out of it. Cousin of mine's a reporter, General. All it needs is one word. Just one word to trigger things off. The word "massacre", for instance. That'd do.' He half-turned his head. 'You, uh . . . get my drift?'

Dempsey breathed inwards through his nose, a long rasping, bubbling sound, medium-pitched in tone. It sounded like someone snorting coke after too long away from it.

'So why don't you just blow the whistle anyway?' he said in a tired voice.

Hardin turned round fully, his hands resting lightly on his hips. His face had lost its colour.

'Because they're dead, General,' he said tightly. 'All

12

lying jumbled up in their shallow graves, arms and legs and heads in silly twisted unnatural positions. By now I should imagine they'll be rotting down nicely, if the ants haven't gobbled them all up. But whatever hideous state they're in, nothing I say or do will bring them back.' He laughed harshly. 'Poetic justice if they did all rise up again, don't you think, General? The march of the dead, crying for vengeance! 900 tattered, rotting, gibbering, shambling figures with but a single mindless urge: tear the guts out of General Ronald Clarke Dempsey. Like those old horror comics I used to read as a kid: *Tales from the Crypt, The Vault of Horror*, junk like that. The bad guy always got it in the end. Always got his in the most monstrous and ugly fashion. Very moral, General. A monstrous reprisal for a monstrous crime. I like that. Because it was a monstrous crime, General, believe me, and it ought not to remain unpunished. But then, hell, we're committing monstrous crimes in this God-forsaken country all day and every day. We all are. Charlie included. Who's to say who's worst? Torture, forced transfer, defoliation, air strikes, scorched earth, indiscriminate crop destruction, collective punishment, rape, massacre. It's all pretty fucking barbaric, isn't it, General. So what's a lousy 900 stiffs amongst that lot? Mere crapola.'

Even as he spoke, he was getting flashes in his mind, a soundless newsreel of faces and figures, of men and women, he'd killed himself over the past six years: in the jungle, in the festering swamps, on landing zones, in city streets; with knife, garotte, grenade, booby-trap, gun, bare hands; silently, noisily, coolly, in a panic-sweat of desperation.

But always he'd survived. Because he was a good killer, a natural killer; had learned this many years ago, long before he'd come to Vietnam. He often wondered whether killing was his sole motivation in life, the one thing that fuelled him. The idea tortured him; only in the jungle was he almost free of it.

But 900? He never wanted to be that good.

He discovered that his arms were stiff and tense, his hands pressing into and gripping through his shirt the hard flesh at his waist. He shrugged, let his hands drop. He

13

walked towards the door.

'So that's the way of it, General,' he said, letting his voice, too, relax. 'Let the folks back in the World wrestle with My Lai; it's enough to be going on with. As for your chestnuts—like I said, get some other guy to haul them out. I pass on that one. Fact is, I pass on anything you have to offer. Just get off my back, and stay off it.'

Hardin walked down the long corridor to the head of the stairs and stopped for a moment, gazing down at the vast entrance hall below. A girl was coming up the staircase towards him. She was dressed in a blue frock and looked astonishingly beautiful. Hardin still couldn't get over this. You walked down Main Street in any small-town American ville and you could count the number of astonishingly beautiful girls on the fingers of one finger. Here, they were all over the damn place. The odd thing was, you never got jaded; at least, Hardin didn't.

The girl reached the head of the stairs and smiled at him. She had white, even teeth and honey-coloured skin. She wore eyeshadow Western-style round her eyes, perfectly applied.

'Fuck-fuck,' she said in a neutral voice.

Hardin sighed.

'You chose the wrong minute of the wrong day of the wrong week,' he said. 'You couldn't have done worse if you'd tried.'

The girl frowned in puzzlement.

'Fuck-fuck,' she said again.

'No fuck-fuck,' said Hardin.

He went down the stairs, through the wide swing doors, and out into the street.

Dempsey, from the window above, watched him go. He was breathing heavily and mopping his face with his handkerchief. He watched Hardin walk to the end of the street, turn left and disappear into Tu Do.

'Little shit,' he muttered. Actually, Hardin was six foot one, but that was beside the point.

Dempsey turned from the window and gazed round the room. There was comfort here, comfort inspired by money. Dempsey thought: I have a lot of loot stashed in a lot of places. How long would it take me to get it all together and

14

get the fuck out? Then he thought: too fucking long.

In any case, getting it all together would foster suspicion in exactly those quarters where he least wanted it fostered, and at that thought he broke out in a sweat again.

He had just about two weeks to deliver that packet, or Chi would start getting very heavy indeed. Okay, so he had to find someone else to make the drop. It had been a mistake to think Hardin would be fooled into it, a tactical error. There must be no more such errors. He must not, for Chrissake, lose his cool.

He turned his thoughts away from the main problem and pondered the secondary one: Hardin.

Hardin knew too much for his own crapping good. And how he'd discovered it, why he'd gone to such lengths to dig it up, was beside the point. He had it, and that was enough. So he was going to have to be taken out. Permanently.

It was going to need some working out, Dempsey thought, but it shouldn't take too long, once he'd broken the back of it. Already he had a nebulous idea at the back of his mind, and by the time he reached the Base it ought to be firmed out. Dempsey, in a potentially catastrophic situation, was a very fast and fluid organiser. He strode to the telephone and dialled.

'Get me Captain Alkine, at the Base.'

The fat, blue-green, noisy, stupid fly had given up on the window. It now droned across the room and circled Dempsey's head a couple of times, then landed on the clean white blotter set in the middle of the table. Dempsey's right hand came up then down again, almost as a reflex action. There was a sharp crack, and Dempsey rubbed the smeared mess off his palm on to the side of his pants.

'Alkine. I'm coming in. Get the current shit-list out and select maybe a dozen names. Have the files ready for when I get there. Guys who are real redundant, know what I mean? Dead-heads. Another thing: Special Forces Colonel by the name of Hardin. John Hardin. He has a cousin back in the World, some kind of reporter. I want to know where this fucker is, and I want to know right fast.' He glanced at his hand and noticed there was still traces of fly on it. He spat quickly, and rubbed some more. 'Jesus, Alkine, how

15

the hell should I know? I'm asking you. Contact our friends; they'll dig it out. Now just get that crapping list out and start reading.'

General Dempsey banged down the phone, reached for his jacket, and headed for the door.

PART ONE

Unlike the rooms of most of those senior officers who worked in the Intelligence, or 'spook', block on the north side of the US tactical air base at Bien Hoa, Dempsey's office was bare and functional. There was a desk, on which were three metal paper-trays, all empty, one ashtray, and a telephone/intercom system; there was a light green filing cabinet; a dark green wastepaper basket; and, under the window which looked out on to a small patch of well-kept lawn, a long glass-fronted bookcase, which contained four or five military manuals, a Roget's Thesaurus, and a lot of space. There were also three straight-backed, armless chairs placed neatly and at regular intervals along one wall, and one chair with arms which was behind the desk. There was nothing else; not even a calendar.

There were no plants on the window-sill, no Japanese prints on the cream-coloured walls, no comfortable settles or armchairs, no colourful floral drapes hanging at the windows, no souvenir knick-knacks standing, sitting or squatting on any of the room's flat surfaces.

All this was not because Dempsey himself was an austere man who disliked personalising his place of work; quite the contrary. It was simply because he was never in the room for more than two days in a fortnight and saw no point in creating a pleasant, homey atmosphere in a place he hardly used.

This severity of tone did have one advantage. It tended to impress high-level visitors from the States—senators, congressmen, and other snoopers—who went away convinced that Dempsey was a man to be reckoned with. 'Real workaholic,' it was agreed, 'a go-getter; no time for Goddamn fripperies.'

He also had an office at the Special Forces headquarters up in Nha Trang, to the north-east, but no one ever visited that, least of all Dempsey himself.

He now sat at his desk, a thin cheroot in his mouth, and heavy horn-rimmed glasses on his beak of a nose. He was tapping the right arm of the chair with a neatly manicured

17

forefinger. To his left was a half-open door through which came the subdued clatter of electric typewriters. The air-conditioning hummed.

Captain Alkine came through the door, carrying several tan-coloured files. He switched these to his left hand and pushed the door shut with his right, the motion causing two of the files to fall to the floor. Alkine bent and picked them up. Dempsey snorted.

'You are a not very smart fucker, Alkine. A smart fucker would have kept a hold on the files with both hands and kicked the door shut with his foot. Back-heeled, for Chrissake.'

Alkine placed the pile of files on the desk, turning them so they faced the way Dempsey was looking. He was a thin man, of medium height, with auburn hair and a faint moustache. He wore rimless glasses, behind which were light blue eyes that stared out at the world rather blankly. His whole air was one of vague indecision. It was a very cleverly cultivated air.

Fixed to each of the files was a card behind a clear plastic window, and on each card was the subject's name, date of birth, rank, and other relevant information, including a brief summary of what he'd done and how he'd been dealt with.

'How many?' said Dempsey.

'A dozen, sir. I thought that would be enough.'

Alkine's voice was as neutral as his expression.

'Should only need eight. Maybe seven.' Dempsey's head came up sharply and he glared at Alkine. 'I'll need a chopper pilot, co-pilot, and two gunners, too. But not this sort of crud.'

Alkine started to move towards the door.

'I'll see . . .'

'Siddown!' barked Dempsey. 'It can keep. These had better be good, Alkine, or I'll have your ass minced. We don't have a hell of a lot of time on this one.'

He shuffled through the files, scanning the information on the cards and muttering to himself. By the end of two minutes he'd discarded five files, which he placed on the floor; the rest he pushed to the centre of the desk.

'Okay, let's stroke these around for a while. See if we can

18

get any jism out of them.'

He pulled the top file towards him and opened it.

'Meeker. Seem to recall hearing about this one. Some kind of gutless little fucking creep.'

He began to read.

The pilot yelled, 'Taking fire! I'm taking fire! I'm hit!' into his throat-mike as plexiglass shards blew back past him and down into the main cabin area, showering the crouching infantrymen.

The gunship lurched and dropped, recovered, rolled sickeningly to one side, then righted itself. The pilot had snapped his glasses down over his eyes against the gale of wind now slamming through the smashed nose, and was barking into his mike again, high on adrenalin.

'Pinto four. This is Pinto four. Charlie just blew my nose for me, but am still operational. Repeat: still operational. Lay some heavy shit on the perimeters, you guys. We still goin' in.'

Above the roar of the rotors could be heard the chatter of automatic gunfire—a high-pitched, clean, stuttering sound that almost every man aboard the Huey recognised. It was a sound they heard most days, in some heavy situation or other. Kalashnikov AK-47. The all-purpose Russian assault rifle Charlie seemed to have in unlimited supplies. You could use it anywhere, any time, on almost anything. You could rip a man in half with it; stop a jeep. You could kill helicopters with it.

'But not this one,' said the pilot, a tall, skinny black from Manhattan, named Frank Marco, 'they sure ain't gonna kill this one. This baby stays in one piece, more or less, because I've given the mother too much tender lovin' care to let those vile bastards take her apart.'

He kicked the right rudder, and the Huey yawed and rose, as tracer from thick undergrowth on the edge of the landing zone far below lanced up and past it.

'They've got MGs down there, yelled the co-pilot.

'Shit, man, they got *everything* down there, an' they throwin' it all at us!'

The LZ was a wide dun-coloured clearing surrounded by dense jungle for the most part, with patchy scrub to the north. In the midst of tall trees, their narrow trunks as bare as picked bones for eighty feet or more, thick smoke drifted sluggishly into the hot, unbroken blue of the sky. At irregular intervals around the perimeter of the cleared circle red flashes starred the sombre greenery, blinking on and off in rapid though uneven succession. Bullets hammered over the Huey's body, some penetrating.

'Those fuckers back at Base better start kicking mud in the air damn soon,' said the co-pilot through cupped hands, 'or you're not gonna be able to sit her down, Marco.'

Marco was wrestling with the cyclic and cursing.

'They hit our rotors, we gonna need a fuckin' Chinook to come in and get us, baby! Yeah, an' then they hit the Chinook outta court, we gonna need the whole fuckin' Air Force to save our ass!'

Somewhere down there—maybe dead, maybe not— were two men, crew of a tiny Loach scout. That was who they were after, and that was who Charlie didn't want them to get. Marco had heard of a similar rescue attempt in bandit country where the whole kit-and-kaboodle had gone right down the tube.

First a Cobra scout had gone down, and a Huey, flown in to pull the survivors out, had gone down too. Another Huey had been sent in, and that had been knocked out. A third Huey had been taken out in mid-air, by a rocket. A big Chinook troop-carrier had landed with thirty men, and Charlie had pulled out all the stops—rockets, mortars, machine guns; they'd even brought up a field gun from somewhere.

That was when Command had shrugged its shoulders and muttered stuff like 'collective firepower with ultra-extreme prejudice'. What that meant was there was really no point in wasting more men in what was clearly a pretty hopeless situation. If the survivors made it out of the trap in one piece, fine; if they didn't—well, they were all brave fellows, worth a mention in dispatches.

A sudden heavy explosion below rocked the circling chopper, the blast sending it canting away to one side. In the main cabin a grunt lost his grip on the support rail and yelled in terror as he slithered across the plexiglass-strewn floor towards the open doorway, only prevented from plunging right out by the door-gunner letting go his M-60 and grabbing him by the collar.

'You want to watch your ass, boy,' advised the gunner.

On the other side of the doorway, Lieutenant Paul Meeker, watching this, felt his mouth go dry. Fear was a knife with a serrated edge, twisting and turning in his stomach.

No, not fear. Panic.

Under his combat suit his body was slick with running sweat. He felt he was marinating slowly, almost to the point where he was starting to dissolve. His heavy flak jacket and the intense heat of the day—only slightly alleviated by the gale howling through the chopper's nose—had nothing at all to do with this.

Across from him his squad were combat-ready. He knew that; recognised the way their bodies were angled in expectation. The fact that Charlie was trying to knock them out of the sky—had already nearly blown the gunship to hell—made no difference. Once down, they'd be out of the chopper in seconds, fanning out in well-drilled skirmish line, firing from the hip, hosing down the nearest sector of jungle to them.

They were eager, all of them. Eager to kill; to waste Charlie. He could see it in their eyes, the way they were breathing.

Even Kulitz, the little grunt who'd nearly taken a dive into a thousand feet of nothing. He hadn't moved back to his original place with the rest of the squad, but was crouched beside the door-gunner, who was now back in position and pumping short professional bursts of M-60 fire down at the LZ.

Kullitz, like the rest of them, wanted to get out there.

The fact was, thought Meeker, not one of these idiots has the imagination of an ant.

Didn't they realise what it was like to get a bullet through the guts, or through the chest, or the head? That moment of searing, scalding agony as a lump of metal slammed straight into you, severing arteries, ploughing through bone, ripping into delicate tissue structure. The horror of lying twisted on the ground clawing at yourself as your life-blood pumped powerfully through clutching fingers. Hadn't they ever thought about this?

Meeker had, often. Lately, he'd thought about nothing else.

He'd thought about being shot in the stomach, in the arms, in the legs. He'd imagined sprinting across a rice paddy and a machine gun suddenly opening up in front of him, so that at one moment he was running straight into its line of fire and the next he was being bundled backwards, arms flailing, as his legs were scythed from under him. He'd dreamed of getting caught in cross-fire in the jungle— from all directions, the way Charlie laid on an ambush situation these days—and getting crucified momentarily in mid-air, bullets from all sides cutting him apart. He'd even fantasised slugs from his own mutinous grunts ripping into him (his back, kidneys, spinal column).

But his worst waking, and sleeping, nightmare was a scenario of pure terror—the shot that crippled (lower left leg, maybe) out in bandit country, with the entire squad dead around him, and only him left alive.

And the the little yellow men in black pajamas with their AK-47s would run up and spot him—and kill him slowly, one shot at a time, savouring each round as it was pumped into flesh. Blow his hands off first, then his feet, them move up the legs to the thighs, one shot at a time, the hips, the genitals, one in the stomach, and then maybe concentrate on the arms and shoulders for a while before going back to the lower ribs and the abdomen.

Maybe you'd pass out long before that; maybe you wouldn't. The human frame was a funny thing.

He'd seen guys in the medicentre with arms blown off and legs dangling from mere shreds of bloody gristle, and yet still they'd been conscious—grey-faced and eyes rolling, and hoarse, whining noises bubbling out of their gaping mouths. Christ only knew what they were feeling.

No. Wrong. *He* knew what they were feeling.

He could imagine exactly—it was sharply etched in his mind to the point where he could actually experience it himself—that pain that was beyond pain that was lancing through their nervous systems.

And yet these stupid, mindless robots across the cabin from him were eager to get out there; eager to throw themselves straight into that storm of tissue-tearing,

23

cartilage-rupturing rounds.

And it wasn't as though they knew what they were doing. It wasn't as though they cared about the guys they were supposed to be rescuing. It wasn't even as though they were doing it for the flag.

Jesus, the flag! Most of them wouldn't think twice about using the flag to wipe their ass, should the situation arise.

Sweet Christ, the only reason they were jumping out of this gunship and into that firestorm was because they were *stupid*!

The momentary burst of rage dulled back to fear again. Meeker was not anti-war, or anti-army. In fact, back in the States, at officer school, he'd shown an above-average grasp of the concepts of army life and the techniques of warfare.

He'd shown intelligence in mock-firefights and skill in his deployment of men, and imagination (but not too much) in creating positive combat situations. He was an Alpha student, without being Alpha-Plus.

Nor was he anti-Vietnam in any philosophical or political sense. There were no ideological reasons behind his terror at all.

There was just terror.

It had started when he'd landed at Da Nang from Okinawa just two weeks back. That was when a sniper had taken out the guy standing next to him, near the Base perimeter. They hadn't been off the plane—a big, bulky C-130—more than 20 minutes, and Meeker hadn't even heard the shot above the hubbub of disembarking grunts, movement of supplies and the roar of the aircraft's engine.

But suddenly the guy had keeled over sideways, without a sound, bumping into Meeker and knocking him to the ground, and the first thing Meeker knew that anything was wrong—that the guy hadn't suddenly fainted from the heat, or had an epileptic fit, or was chuggalug drunk—was when he heard someone screaming at him to get his ass into a foxhole, and he discovered he had bits of the guy's head splashed down his fatigues; mostly blood and brains, but flecks of bone too.

That, thought Meeker, was reality. There might be a one in a thousand chance of a fatality in the mock-battles back at

24

training-school, but over here, in Vietnam, the odds were down to one in ten. Or less.

Suddenly, rolling desperately towards the nearest foxhole, the blood of the shot man smearing into the dust on the tarmac, Meeker began to think about getting killed. He began to think that *he* could get killed.

That was when the terror started.

'I can see 'em, Lieutenant!'

Meeker came out of his dream. It was the M-60 gunner, a tall blond from the Mid-West, with a thick moustache. He was jabbing at the landing area below with his right hand.

Near a patch of thick undergrowth, lying half-hidden behind some scrub, were two figures in camouflage suits. One was waving.

'Saw a movement in the undergrowth and thought it was Charlie, so I gave it a burst. They came running out and flopped down. It's them, okay. Lucky I over-shot the fuckers.'

Meeker wondered what was lucky about it. If the M-60 gunner had nailed them, they wouldn't have to go down and do the pickup, but could get the hell out of here and back to Base.

Up front, Captain Frank Marco sent the chopper swooping down towards the ground.

'Charlie ain't seen 'em. We're in with a chance, Marco.'

'Fuckin'-A. Still ain't gonna be no picnic, baby. Where's the heavy stuff from Base? Those outrageous fuckers ought to start earnin' their bread.'

As if on cue, the ground below began to erupt in angry flashes of flame and black smoke. Shells screamed overhead and thundered amongst the tall trees, shattering them, hurling long strips of living timber into the air like flying javelins.

Marco whooped with glee.

'Cream the yellow peril, you guys! Okay, Lieutenant— it's all yours!'

The Huey circled the landing zone once, then sailed in towards where the two figures were now crouching and firing back into the undergrowth behind them. As it fell towards the group, two massive explosions ripped the earth apart nearby, the shock-wave bowling over the two fugitives, and slamming the chopper to one side viciously.

'Shitbirds!' screamed Marco into his throat-mike. 'You fuckers'll kill us all!'

He was now committed to a landing, but had to wrestle with the controls to settle the chopper against the earth at a distance from his target. About 500 yards, he figured; which was better than a thousand, but still a hairy distance.

'Go get 'em, Meeker!' he bawled.

Meeker, in the main cabin, was in a daze. He could hear the slowing *wap-wap-wap* of the rotors, and could see, outside the door, what looked like acres of flattened grass. He could just make out the target—the two men—firing into the jungle, one using an M-16, the other (probably the pilot) a handgun. He could smell sweat and oil and the tang of steel. He could feel his radio-man scrabbling at his sleeve; his sergeant nudging him.

But he couldn't move an inch.

'Out!' roared the sergeant, glaring savagely at Meeker. 'Get out there and raise the shit-level!'

He went past Meeker and jumped down, the rest of the men following him fast and fanning out, hunched figures pumping rounds at the wall of greenery surrounding them.

'Sir?' It was the radio-man, white-faced and little more than a kid. 'We gotta go . . .'

Meeker nodded abruptly, pushed him out of the Huey.

'Stay with Sergeant Aikman. Tell him I'm coming now.'

Meeker turned on his heel, aware that the door-gunner was watching him with a startled expression on his face. This didn't bother him. He knew precisely what he had to do.

He stepped up into the pilot's area, his .45 automatic in his hand. He couldn't remember unbuttoning the stiff leather holster to take the weapon out; hadn't even been aware he was holding it until he stepped into the upper cabin. Little things like that didn't matter.

He waved the gun at Marco.

'Up,' he said. 'Lift off. Get us out of here.'

The co-pilot's mouth dropped open.

'What the fuck. . . ?'

Marco held the cyclic tightly. He knew exactly what had happened and, unless he handled the situation right, exactly what was going to happen. The automatic was inches from his head but he grinned, showing startlingly white teeth.

'Couple of seconds, Lieutenant, then we all gonna be going home. You take a seat in the . . .'

'Up,' said Meeker. 'I'm sorry, sir, but we have to move off. Now.'

'Sure, Lieutenant, we'll do that. We'll lift off. Sure . . .'

As Marco was talking he was smiling at Meeker, and his right boot was nudging his co-pilot's leg. The co-pilot's face was beaded with sweat. On the other side of his seat was a monkey-wrench.

His fingers touched it while Marco talked on, and curled round it. He gripped it, tensed, swung round fast. The monkey-wrench caught on a projection, clanged with the impact, was half-jerked from his hand. The co-pilot screamed '*Shit!*', scrabbling to keep a hold on the weapon—and Meeker turned slightly and shot him through the head.

The co-pilot was slammed sideways as the bullet took him just behind the left ear, ploughing on through the back of his head and smashing into what remained of the plexiglass dome. Blood sprayed over the controls in front.

Marco jumped up from his seat, and then collapsed back with a choked grunt as Meeker turned again, slamming the barrel of the automatic into his jaw, tearing the flesh almost to the bone.

In the main cabin, the door-gunner yelled '*Hey!*' and jumped towards the pilot's area.

Meeker swung in a half-circle and fired. It was almost point-blank range, with the tall blond, framed in the opening, a target a blind man couldn't have missed.

The bullet took the gunner in the chest and punched him backwards, turning him over in a back-flip before he crashed to the floor. He didn't even scream. Meeker briefly took in the man's shocked expression, the vivid crimson puddle he was lying in, then turned back to Marco.

'Get it up.'

'You off your fuckin' head, Lieutenant.'

'Better do as I say, sir.'

'Look, Meeker, we can work this out. We'll say Charlie

hit these two. Ain't gonna be no post mortems with all this shit flyin' round. I can get you a job in the rear. I got friends. Easiest fuckin' thing in the world. So it's your first mission out. So your nerve's shot to shit. So it's happening all over. So what the hell.'

'My nerve hasn't gone, sir. I'm perfectly aware of what I'm doing. I'm getting out in one piece.'

'They gonna have your balls for this, baby.'

'Better move it, sir. We don't have much time.'

Marco's face was expressionless as he turned to the controls.

'Fuckin'-A.'

Out in the field, Sergeant Aikman was kneeling behind a stunted thorn bush, firing at a patch of undergrowth where, seconds before, he'd seen a movement.

All around him was the sound of frenzied combat. The staccato stutter of his men's M-16s; the heavier chatter of machine gun fire; the thump of shells in the trees; yells and cries. Something else, too. Something that sounded out of place.

The racket of the gunship's rotors, peaking up to lift-off pitch.

Aikman, horrified, half-rose and turned, screamed out as the chopper rose above him and swept up into the sky.

He started running, still screaming, and machine gun bullets cut his legs from under him and stitched a bloody pattern across his back. As he stopped screaming, others started.

On the far side of the landing zone small groups of black-clad figures could be seen emerging from the jungle, firing from the hip.

Watching all this from the chopper, Meeker lit a cigarette one-handed. The barrel of the automatic in his left hand rested on Marco's shoulder, the nose lined up with the black's right ear. The scene below receded from sight as the gunship sailed over the green tree-tops.

Meeker blew smoke out of his mouth; relaxed.

'No one's going to put any damn bullets into me, Captain,' he said conversationally.

*   *   *

Dempsey closed the file and slid it away from him. The cheroot in his mouth had gone out, and he pinched the blackened end over the ashtray and rubbed it with thumb and forefinger. Shreds of charred leaf and dead ash fell on to the glass surface. He relit the cheroot and sucked and puffed until the tip glowed red.

'How long ago was this fucker sentenced?'

Alkine, wise in the ways of General Ronald Clarke Dempsey, knew better than to point out that the date was on the card stuck to the front of the file. He knew the date, in any case. He had a memory like a card-index, which was precisely why he was where he was now.

'Six days ago, sir.'

Dempsey grunted through his nose. He took off his glasses and half-turned, holding them up towards the window. What he saw there seemed to satisfy him. He put them back on again.

'You ever out in the field, Alkine?'

'No, sir.'

'No combat experience, huh?'

'None whatsoever, General.'

Dempsey cackled with laughter.

'Same like me, Alkine. No crapping combat experience whatso-crapping-ever.'

Alkine knew this. Just as he knew that Dempsey was well aware that he had no combat experience. Often you had to humour Dempsey; make him comfortable in his role of The Boss ... The Head Honcho ... The Man With The Power. It was something at which Alkine was particularly adept, and was another reason why he was where he was now.

'We know how to look after Number One, eh, Alkine?'

'Sure do, General.'

'And you don't need crapping combat experience for that.'

Still chuckling, Dempsey pulled the second file towards him and opened it.

COLBY

The trees were dripping blood.

That came as a hell of a shock to Colby; a cosmic blast. He hadn't noticed anything out of the ordinary until the moment he recognised the red, viscous fluid for what it was.

He'd been too preoccupied with his own private high.

Colby was shot through with acid. It was coming out of his ears, eyes, mouth and nose. Probably out of the pores of his skin, too. Probably out of his anus, if the truth were known. The only problem was—and this Colby didn't know—he was shot through with bad acid.

The M-16 in his hands felt as light as a feather-duster; lighter, in fact. Any moment now it was going to take off and float up to Mars. Or maybe Venus. Or maybe right out of the Solar System altogether; gathering speed as it journeyed on into the unplumbed, untextured depths of space and time—the first M-16 in recorded history to travel at the speed of light. That was worth thinking about.

On the other hand, there were a thousand million other things worth thinking about, too. Like the last R-and-R in Saigon; that gas station in Arizona where the one-armed attendant juggled Indian clubs as a sideshow; ice-cold Coke straight from the fridge, with beads of moisture clinging to the bottle; Corporal Macey getting blown to shit when he went to take a leak in the bushes and tripped over a mine; that Big Brother concert just before he'd come out, with the crazy singer, Janis something-or-other, throwing her tits all over the stage; the time he'd whupped that shitbird creep Saccetti out in the desert in his old man's Chevvy; the pile of Batman comicbooks he'd picked up for cents in the local Salvation Army and sold for dollars to the nut in Memphis; solid silver dog-tags with your astrological sign on them the freak in Da Nang was touting; the way every time his feet hit the ground red and green stars burst in the air . . .

And that was no lie, thought Colby. Hell, this jungle was getting weirder and weirder: a dazzling light show of freaky effects. It looked like Charlie was getting sophisticated.

Maybe this was some sort of strange, far-out signalling system gauged to keep in time with the patrol's march-step? Or maybe—and this just went to show how sneaky the slant-eyed little fuckers were getting—it was gauged to keep in time with *his* march-step? Maybe they were zeroing in on *him*?

One thing was for sure in this crazy business, a PG-7 grenade from a rocket launcher at close range'd sure fuck up *his* health record.

Colby, head down and eyes flicking to right and left in nervous expectation, moved on through the clinging riot of vines and creepers, his boots alternately thudding down on to soil or squelching into rotting vegetation. Tiny insects buzzed and hummed around his face, every few seconds launching suicide attacks at his eyes.

But he was used to that. You got used to stuff like that after a year out here. You got used to it after a month, actually. It got so that incidents like that didn't bother you at all. The only thing that bothered you was staying alive and in one piece. Especially in one piece.

'Keep it moving up the line! *Hey, Colby!* Get the lead outta your boots! You think this is a stroll in the park we're on, *numbnuts*? You want I should give you my arm, *fuck-head*? Spaced-out fucking' panty-waist *sackashit*, the only thing you'll get from me is a kick in the balls, scumbag, less you *move it on*!'

That was Sergeant Marler. Sonuvabitch. A real redneck motherfucker from way back when. What Sergeant Marler needed was a phoz grenade up his ass, and the guy that tossed it ought to get a medal.

Colby wondered why Sergeant Marler was such a piece of shit. He wondered if Marler's old man was a piece of shit. Maybe all the Marlers were a piece of shit going right back to Dan'l Boone. How in hell did Marler's wife put up with it? Did he call her scumbag? Or numbnuts? Well, no; maybe not numbnuts. That wouldn't really apply, her being a woman and all.

Colby tried to think of something that would apply to a woman, that Sergeant Marler might use, but couldn't come up with anything. Not even the mildest obscenity. It wasn't worth pounding the brain about, anyhow. But at least it took his mind off all that blood . . .

Jesus, there it was again: a positive stream of red stuff cascading down from the forest ceiling high above. Red and thick and sticky-looking.

What it had to be was the end-product of some kind of really wild ambush that must have taken place only minutes before. Luke the Gook had some pretty far-out ways of killing people: arrow-traps; stakes in the ground with fire hardened points covered with buffalo shit; heavy mud balls with spikes all over them that swung down when released and took your head off. All that shit.

What must have happened here was a patrol walking into a whole bunch of concealed *nooses*, lying on the jungle floor. You put your foot in one and *Zap!* Next thing you knew you were yanked into the air and heading for the wild blue yonder like Superman. Is it a bird, is it a plane? No, it's just some poor fucking grunt who's about to have his cheques cashed in. That had to be the answer.

Okay. The guys would all be zooming top-of-the-tree-wards, and Charlie's up there, waiting to catch them. Probably they'd each be using some kind of catcher's glove to grab the flying grunts as they popped up and pull 'em in, on to a handy branch. Then the slaughter would start.

To keep the noise level down, they'd obviously have to use knives, or icepicks, or butchers' cleavers to finish 'em off. No mileage in using guns; the shooting would be heard all over the jungle. Yeah, it *had* to be meat-axes. Charlie'd really get off on that, hacking a US grunt into prime cuts. And then —*Right!*—having torn out all the good-luck emblems (hearts, livers, lungs, kidneys, scrotal bags and such) they'd simply leave what was left to drip gore down on to the jungle below. *As a warning!*

All ye who enter here, *Watch your ass!*

Jesus galloping Christ, though Colby, this is getting heavier and heavier. He remembered some guy had told him of a chalked-up notice outside of Khe Sanh after the 77-day siege at Tet. It simply read 'All Yankees who read this will be killed.'

The smart thing about it was that the piece of wood on which the notice was scrawled was large, but the writing itself was small. Almost unreadable at four or five paces even. So naturally guys went right up to it, crowding round to see what was written there, and the sniper who'd positioned himself on the other side had himself a Goddamn field day! *Zip, zip, zip!* Must've finished off a score or more before they smoked the little fucker out. *Really* smoked him, too. The guy was up a tree, they set fire to it; burned it right down with a can of napalm. That sure as Hell roasted *his* chestnuts.

Yup, that was what all this blood was, no doubt about it. A warning. Death awaits you, Yankee fuckers! Proceed no further! God, this was really heavy . . .

'Colby, I ain't tellin' you again, smackhead! Move your boots or I'll burn your ass with a flame-gun! Goddamn freakhead *dungbrain!*'

Colby couldn't make up his mind which was worse, the blood pouring from the trees or Sarge Marler howling like a werewolf—*Right!* That was it! Exactly like a werewolf! A kind of strange, echoing ululation that bounced around the stone corridors of his mind. It was absolutely *weird!*

Those star-flashes were getting bigger, too.

And changing colour, damn it. Not just read and green, but yellow, blue, white, all the shades of the fucking rainbow. Charlie was bombarding them with technicolour fire-balls. Except there was no heat and no noise. This was absolutely a new twist, but why in hell was no one commenting on the utter strangeness of the experience? Surely everyone in the patrol could see what was happening? Jesus, thought Colby, you'd think they'd all been turned into zombies.

Up ahead, just moving out of sight round a bend in the trail, was Lucasz, head bent, back slightly hunched, M-16 held in both hands. Lucasz was a friendly guy; Colby owed him cigarettes. This could be a way of paying off the debt: warn him of the danger; point out that since the VC were blasting them with this crazy new weapon he ought to know about it. God alone knew what these cool soundless fireballs were doing to a guy. Maybe they were sending out gamma rays that turned you impotent, or something? Wilder things than that had happened in this insane conflict.

Colby moved round the bend and gazed at the scene in front of him. He froze.

Jesus! This couldn't be happening! *This simply could not be happening!*

There was a Goddamn VC calmly slitting Lucasz's throat with a knife that looked to be as big as a fucking bayonet! Colby had never seen a knife that was so big before. It was immense! Huge! And *sharp*! That blade was just sinking into Lucasz's jugular and slicing his whole fucking head off. Like it was a peach, or something! This was utterly *bizarre*!

But what the hell to do? Too late to help Lucasz; he was beyond all aid, his spirit already merging into the infinite. And there was no doubt that a quick burst of M-16 fire would do far more damage than anything else Colby could imagine. Why, it'd bring those gore-splashed VC down from the tree-tops, for sure. *There'd be a fucking massacre!*

He had to play it cool; play it by ear. The VC didn't seem to have realised he'd come round the bend; maybe Mayerhold, behind, would know what to do?

Colby carefully twisted round. Mayerhold was just turning the corner—only it wasn't Mayerhold at all. It was a VC in Mayerhold's uniform!

God in heaven! This was undoubtedly the most appalling situation he'd ever experienced. The VC were knocking off the guys in the patrol one by one—infiltrating the platoon in a totally heinous and rotten way. It was really Goddamn *sneaky*!

Luckily, the VC behind hadn't noticed that Colby had spotted him. Colby turned to his front again, and nodded grimly to himself. The dirty dog who'd slit Lucasz's throat had somehow gotten rid of the body and was now wearing Lucasz's combat fatigues, holding Lucasz's Armalite, and, indeed, looking remarkably like Lucasz himself. Clearly, a master of disguise—except for those *slant eyes*. That was the giveaway. That, and the smile. Lucasz-VC was smiling, and this teeth were filling the jungle—great blocks of ivory that danced and jigged through the undergrowth in time with the kaleidoscope star-flashes; and that of course was the solid connection. The teeth and the star-bursts were linked; they emanated from one source, and one only:

34

Victor fucking Charles.

Damn it, but this had to be the dirtiest way of fighting a war since the night-attack was invented.

It all fell into place. The blood pouring down from the tree-tops was the signal for those VC on the ground to get in on the action with this new patrol. Those star-flashes—well, it was obvious. Some kind of far-out hypnotic device that totally zapped the mind of the guys in the patrol so they didn't cry out when Charlie came at 'em with his big knife. A swift change of clothes, and very soon the patrol would become a totally VC fighting force—*in grunt fatigues*!

That was the sheer ingenuity of the plan. Probably, there was some ulterior motive behind all this: a march on Saigon, a quisling infiltration of Da Nang; something like that. The overall concept didn't matter; it wasn't important. What was important was that he'd spotted the outrageous scheme before they could get to *him*.

Not that this was going to do him much good. There was no way out now; no hope for him but to go down fighting like a man. It was forty to one, but at least he had the element of surprise on his side.

Colby chuckled, lifted his gun. Lucasz-VC had his back to him again, and in front were maybe a half dozen men, all, naturally, VC. Colby's finger squeezed the Armalite's trigger, and giant red darts leapt from the muzzle of the gun, knocking the VC over in an orderly sequence, like a pack of leaning cards. Too bad about those little monkeys waiting above. With a bit of luck, he could maybe wipe out this bunch on the ground before they came swooping down on their lianas, whooping and hollering like Tarzan of the Apes. Which would merely add to the whooping and hollering that had already started down here; just shove the decibel level up a little, was all.

Colby swung right round and dropped to his knees, still firing. Just in time, by Christ! They'd come up on him while he'd been busy and it looked like they were massing for the attack. All the better! He kept squeezing the trigger and stuff was spraying out of the gun that had no business to be down the Goddamn barrel at all. Long streams of red and white plastic chips that said PAPAPAPAPAPA in block letters and extremely loud tones. Still, there was no doubt that it was effective. Guys were yelling with laughter and swimming away from him through the air: a kind of fast butterfly backstroke in slow motion. And someone was trying to tear his throat out by applying really extravagant pressure on it and screaming at him in words as big as skyscrapers and the darkness must be the sun going down—

*   *   *

'That's about as much as I can stomach on this one,' grated Dempsey, flipping the file shut. 'That's the sort of crot we're getting in this man's army now, Alkine. Goddamn weirdos and junkheads. Was a time,' he jabbed a chunky forefinger in Alkine's direction, 'when all you had to do was get yourself a fucking speeding-ticket, and the army wouldn't look at you. Wouldn't even spit at you. That was when Ike was on the throne. I look back on those days with a great deal of regret.'

Captain Alkine nodded soberly. Dempsey was a hard man when it came to drugs of any description. He might peddle them—and frequently did if the money was right and the deal was hygienic—but he hated the people who used them, and he never used them himself. At all. It was Dempsey's boast that he depended on no one, and no thing.

The irony was, Alkine thought, that for all his bluster Dempsey depended heavily on him, and didn't know it. Dempsey was a smart operator right enough, but he still needed someone to do the dirty work: make the phone calls, transfer the files, organise the pickups, sweeten the natives. Only as a last resort would Dempsey really get his own hands soiled.

'Must've been some Goddamn bad trip,' said Dempsey, polishing his glasses.

'It was later established, General, that Colby had taken an impure derivative of lysergic acid commonly known as LBJ.'

Dempsey's thick eyebrows rose.

'LBJ?'

'Yes, sir. I understand the sales pitch is "guaranteed a

36

bummer'', sir.'

'Colby can vouch for that. Seems he blew away half his own patrol before some guy managed to take him out.' Dempsey tapped the thin file. 'According to this trial report he was raving for a couple of days back at Base.'

Alkine fought back a yawn that was threatening to stretch his mouth muscles to their utmost limits. Outside the weather was sultry, but the room's air-conditioning took care of that. Alkine could see, across the lawn, an Air Force dog-handler walking a Doberman. The dog was pissing against a signpost, and the handler was standing beside him, gazing into the air as though something extremely important was happening 5000 feet up.

'Guaranteed a bummer, huh?' mused Dempsey. 'Maybe we'll let Colby write a testimonial for the guys who're marketing the junk. Then again, maybe we won't. Maybe we'll just sling his freaky, doping, goofus ass into this operation. He's sure as fuck a perfect candidate, because the way I figure it this deal's guaranteed an A-1 bummer.'

The phone buzzed; Dempsey reached out and flipped a switch.

'Yeah?'

'Lucas Dowling, General.'

'Hold him.'

Dempsey pushed the switch back up and smiled fatly.

'Not Luke the Gook, Alkine, but Luke the Spook. Could be our friends have already gotten something on that wise-ass Hardin's cousin. If they have,' the smile disappeared, as though wiped off with a rag, 'you know exactly what to do.'

Alkine nodded and made for the door. Dempsey picked up the third file.

At night, the cell was just about bearable. The temperature was around 85°, which compared favourably with the midday high that often reached furnace-like proportions.

Worse than the heat, though, was the stench, but O'Mara, squatting bare-foot amidst his own filth, had long since grown accustomed to that. It didn't bother him now. He'd even gotten used to the swarms of flies that descended on him from dawn to dusk and often covered him completely—a ceaselessly shifting, rippling blanket of hungry questing insects.

At first it had nearly driven him crazy—much to the amusement of Captain Baines who, despite the stink of human excrement (or maybe, O'Mara sometimes thought, because of it) spent hours watching him through the tiny barred window in the cell door—but after three days of almost mind-snapping harassment, out of sheer self-preservation he'd begun to experiment. Begun to coax what he'd never been told about but which is the exclusive privilege of every human being—the power of the will—into life. He started to force himself to relax, let the insects buzz and crawl all over his sweat-drenched face and body. After a while he found to his surprise that forcing himself to relax was no longer a conscious effort; he could do it automatically. He could forget about the insects and the smell and the heat; it was as though they did not exist. This revelation turned him to thinking about his mind: what it could do, where it could go.

Soon he could lie down on the stinking (that is, non-smelling) floor and within a minute or so be, to all intents and purposes, asleep. His mind wasn't in the cell, anyhow, and that was the main thing.

Baines hadn't liked that. Mental escape was the same as physical escape in his book. At first he'd come in every so often and clubbed O'Mara awake with his stick. But that disturbed the flies, who transferred their attentions to Baines while he was in the cell. Baines hadn't liked that either.

One way out was to hook O'Mara up on a short-length chain, so he had to squat against the wall with his hands held up against the concrete, as though someone was menacing him with a gun.

That had been smart of Baines and hell for O'Mara. But only for the first day or so. Then the tall, skinny black had been able to dip into his self-induced trancelike state again, even in that position, and the flies had ceased to bother him.

Finally Baines had tired of the game and let him out on the long chain during the day. He'd gone back to what he personally considered the best way—the tried and true method—of humiliating his victim. Regular beatings.

O'Mara was in the brig because he'd lost his cool.

O'Mara rarely lost his cool. He was an easy-going dude from Alabama who, before the draft hit him, had been a session-man in the Fame Studios at Muscle Shoals. He played slide-guitar and at one time or another had backed King Curtis, Aretha Franklin, Wilson Pickett. He'd gigged with a lot of guys; sat in twice with Clapton.

The circle he moved in was easy-going too. Black or white, yellow or red. Made no difference. The important thing was how you worked your chops. How you turned it on. How you laid it down.

O'Mara laid it down good, and he was getting better.

Getting hit by the draft was a mean fucker; meanest fucker he'd ever experienced. But if you stayed cool and kept your eyes open out on patrol and didn't get too sassy with Honky two-stripers (who tended more to be racist sons of bitches than three-stripers, for some weird reason), there was an evens chance of getting out alive and back to blowing up a storm in the studios.

But O'Mara hadn't stayed cool.

He was in the brig; had been for what seemed like months. At times he couldn't rightly recall exactly why he was in this special brig on the outskirts of Saigon. Something about refusing to do latrine duty for the twentieth time and breaking the arm of the corporal who'd tried to duck him in the piss-bucket. Something like that. It all seemed so long ago. In any case, it wasn't a memory he particularly wanted to hold on to. Far better to think about the time he'd done a gig with Duane Allman and the way they'd traded choruses on Willie Dixon's 'Shake For Me' for fifty minutes, after hours.

The way things were now, though, it didn't look like he'd ever tickle his axe again.

O'Mara opened his eyes and looked at his fingers. Once they'd been long, slender, sensitive; on his guitar he could talk with them. Now they were thick and sausage-like; broken and torn; crusted with dried blood.

O'Mara couldn't figure out how Captain Baines had discovered he was a guitarist. It must have been a hell of a charge when he did, though. Hell of a charge.

'Hear you play guitar, boy. That right?'

Baines hadn't bothered waiting for an answer. By that time O'Mara hadn't spoken a word in two weeks.

'A fine way of making a living, boy. Seems like you're in luck. Could be this'll put you in my good books. My ole daddy used to like a good guitar-plucker fucker, and no doubt my own high regard for the instrument stems from this fact. My daddy held Ukelele Ike in high esteem, but me, I'm a mite more up to date. What I like is C-and-W, boy. There's a lotta heart there. It's the music of the people, boy, as I expect you'll agree. You don't? You don't agree? You don't even like Country music, boy? You are meaning to tell me that you are of the opinion that such giants as my hero Jim Reeves, and that fine, melodious musician Hank Williams have about as much talent as these here buzzing insects that seem to have taken such a shine to you?'

Baines had shaken his head, a grotesque mask of baffled puzzlement creasing his fat face.

'You surprise me, boy. Fact is, you sadden, not to say disgust me. I got a feeling, boy, that what you care for is that shitty ole nigra blues crap. And if that's the case, as I suspect it is, I have to say that I have to do something to stop the rot. Because the fewer folk that play that shitty ole nigra blues crap, the sweeter our dear homeland will be. The sound of it's soiling the very air itself. And there's only one way to stop it, boy, as you'll very shortly discover . . .'

Baines, grinning, had swung his stick.

Baines's stick was a cross between a cop's night-stick and a baseball bat, slightly tapering at one end towards a handle. Baines carried it everywhere; was never seen without it. He was forever cleaning and polishing it lovingly with a scrap of oily rag, especially after an evening session with O'Mara.

'Got to keep it nice, boy. Make sure all the dents smooth out.'

But that was some time after the first blow had slammed into O'Mara's fingers, splayed upwards on the concrete wall.

Baines had been systematic, O'Mara had to give him that. He'd smashed the stick into the right hand three times, then paced slowly round the black's twitching figure before repeating the dosage across his left hand. Then he'd walked back round and started over on the right hand.

After the first fierce wash of agony had speared down his arms, it seemed to O'Mara as though his fingers had simply gone numb. Then he started to feel the pain, as Baines struck out again and again, chuckling as he pounded the slender fingers into a bloody pulp. It was horrifying, as though someone were ramming shards of glass into the joints of his knuckles and twisting them around.

He'd tried desperately not to scream. He'd hissed out his agony through clenched teeth, his chest heaving, his back straining against the roughness of the concrete. Then he couldn't hold it back any longer. He'd lost sight of the cell; all he could see was a scarlet haze, boiling and rolling like smoke before his eyes. Then his mouth had dropped open, and he'd bellowed '*No!*'

Baines had stopped.

'First time you've shown you weren't dumb in quite a while, boy. Good to hear the sound of another voice in here. Hurts my jaw to keep yakkity-yakking all the time.'

He'd taken his rag from the hook on the door and started to wipe the stick, grimacing and tutting in mock-irritation.

'Jesus! All this dirty nigra blood. Don't clean off as well as white man's blood, boy. Don't know why. Must be something alien in the mix. Don't know what you're going to do about them ole black digits of yours. They're not looking so damn good. Tell you what, boy.' Baines had stopped what he was doing and had leaned over O'Mara, his voice soft, his tone confidential. 'Piece of advice. What you might well do is start playing with yourself. Get my meaning? Start playing with that big ole black member of yours. Harden it up a little. See what I'm getting at? Then curve your fingers round that thick ole solid nigra stalk, and shape them digits up a little.'

Even through the haze of pain that clouded his mind O'Mara had felt a faint flicker of fear finger him, as he began to realise exactly where Captain Baines was at.

And afterwards, when the fat little man had gone, and O'Mara had forced the agony of his broken fingers back into the furthest corners of his mind, he'd begun to rationalise the situation.

O'Mara knew plenty of gays; one had been a member of a band he'd gotten together for a couple of gigs in Huston. Nice guy; good musician. Frankly, O'Mara didn't give a shit if a guy was gay or straight, so long as he was cool.

Baines wasn't gay. Not in the accepted sense. And he sure as hell wasn't cool. Baines was a sadist—some kind of monstrous weirdo who got off on pain. Amongst other things. Christ alone knew what was going on in the dark caverns of his mind.

All O'Mara knew was that he didn't have a lot of time left. A week; maybe a couple of weeks. That was all. Because Baines was slowly losing whatever strange inhibition he had that stopped him from seeking an overt sexual confrontation.

And now, as he squatted in the darkening cell, and heard the sound of Baines's footsteps coming along the passageway outside, O'Mara knew his time was up.

Baines was drunk. That was easy to tell. He was shambling, his footsteps uncertain, irregular. It took him a long time to put the key in the lock and get the door open. He almost fell into the cell, muttering and cursing as he grabbed at the door to steady himself.

O'Mara had never seen Baines drunk before.

Baines slammed the door shut, and locked it. He was chuckling to himself quietly.

'Jesus! Je-sus . . .'

He pushed himself away from the door and staggered slightly as he came into the meagre light afforded by the tiny window set high in the cell wall. He was wearing lipstick.

It was badly applied, thick on the top lip and part of the lower. The rest was a crooked smear that extended over his sweat-beaded chin. He bent at the waist, swaying slightly as he wagged a thick, stubby forefinger in front of O'Mara's nose.

'Hoo-ee! Jesus. Boy, you are in for a high ole time tonight. A high ole time. No, really.'

He unbuckled his belt, and unthreaded it through the loops of his waist-band. His belly, released from constraint, sagged outwards, and Baines patted it affectionately.

'High ole time. Gonna have me a high ole time, nigra. Gotta get together. That's what they say. Black 'n' white gotta buddy-buddy. Ain't that right? Sure it is. Prettied myself up for you, boy. Gotta look my best.'

He leaned over, holding on to the wall behind O'Mara with one hand and running the fingers of his other hand through the black's hair. Suddenly his grip tightened. He screwed the hair into a knot, dragging O'Mara's head back and to one side.

'You gonna have to be nice to me, boy, 'cos I'm gonna give you a little something to eat. Gonna taste real good, too. A toothsome little morsel. Best you ever tasted, nigra. Is that the truth? Huh?'

He jerked at O'Mara's head.

'Huh?'

'Yeah,' croaked O'Mara.

'Yes, sir,' said Baines softly.

'Yes, sir.'

'Yes, sir, Captain Baines!'

'Yes, sir, Captain Baines.'

Baines leaned down even closer, his whisky-drenched breath gusting into O'Mara's face. He licked his lips.

'So let's get friendly, okay, boy?' he whispered hoarsely. 'Let's get real friendly.'

His tongue flicked out and back again. He let go of the wall and stroked O'Mara's upturned face. He half-closed his eyes.

That was when O'Mara jerked hard on his chains, and the fastening above jumped out of the concrete, smoothly and with almost no sound at all.

Baines eyes shot open. He started to say something, but the chain and fastening fell heavily on to his bowed back, and he gave an astonished grunt. His face turned brick-red and he made to jump back.

O'Mara drove his right knee savagely upwards, burying it in Baines's groin with stunning force, and Baines's eyes squeezed shut as he squealed like a shot hog. O'Mara sprang up like a sprinter off the block, whirling the slack of the chain. The heavy fastening slammed across the fat man's face, cracking the bridge of his nose, tearing skin off like paper, sending blood spurting into the air in a scarlet fountain. Baines, clutching his groin, howled and started to fall backwards, and O'Mara caught his neck with the thin chain, looping it and tugging fiercely. Baines rocked forwards again. He tried to grab at the black's crotch, but O'Mara shifted slightly and brought his knee up hard under Baines's chin with a meaty crack. The fat man's head snapped back, and O'Mara yanked on the chain viciously, tightening it.

He sank down until he was face to face with the groaning man. Spittle bubbled from between Baines's lips; dark blood dripped thickly from his shattered nose, sliding over the lighter crimson of the lipstick and on down his chin, mingling with the sweat and the drooling saliva.

It had been surprisingly easy to work the fastening loose, once O'Mara had set his mind to it. The concrete was soft; they'd used too much sand or something, and probably this lousy climate didn't help. They hadn't plugged the filling properly, either. Looked like the whole jail complex had been erected on the cheap. Anyhow, it had only taken him three days of working at it. Three nights, to be exact. He could have taken Baines any time during the past couple of days, but the fat man hadn't been around.

Now he was right there, in front of him, wheezing and cursing and gobbling and not making an awful lot of sense.

Baines suddenly lunged forward with his head, cracking it hard against O'Mara's brow. The black grunted thickly, shook his head to clear the bursting stars inside it, and loosened his grip long enough to smash the wrist-shackle of his right hand straight between Baines's eyes.

The fat man rocked back again, blubbering and

44

squealing, blood welling up out of the torn gash. O'Mara yanked on the chain once more, tightening it around Baines's thick neck. The steel links bit into his throat, sinking deep into the flesh until they could hardly be seen. Baines's eyes were wide now, pleading; his pudgy hands clawed feebly at the air. Scarlet droplets popped out of his open mouth in thin, almost translucent bubbles as blood vessels ruptured and burst.

O'Mara kept up the pressure for quite some time after Captain Baines's grey eyes had glazed over completely.

*   *   *

Dempsey closed the file with a deep-throated grunt of satisfaction.

So far so good. Alkine was earning his money: this guy O'Mara was a prime candidate for what he had in mind. Who'd ever miss a Goddamn nigger who strangled his jailer in the brig?

Mind you, thought Dempsey, it was clear this Baines character wasn't running a very tight ship, and moreover was some kind of fucking pervert, from what the nigger said. If he could be believed, that is. Dempsey's old man had warned Dempsey never to trust a nigger, and by God the old bastard was right. Dope-smoking bunch of shiftless no-goods. Not quite as useless as the Arvins, but then it was well known that the Arvins were an utterly hopeless case, beyond any sort of redemption whatsoever.

Like this whole crapping country, in fact.

Dempsey sat back in his chair and thought: there is no longer any percentage in this war.

It was a thought that had crossed his mind fleetingly some months before, and had returned again and again, with increasing frequency, so that now there was a measure of respectable solidity about it, as though it had always been there.

A year ago, the US military strength in Vietnam had been well over half a million men. Now Richard Nixon had finally made it to the Presidency, elected on an unbeatable ticket that included a strong promise to de-escalate the war.

Well, Nixon was a tricky fucker and Dempsey admired

him for being so. A candidate for the executive office makes a hell of a lot of promises he doesn't intend to keep, and it was a smart move to toss a few sops to the peaceniks. But still and all there *was* a lot of shit flying back home about the war. Maybe too much.

The fact was that 25,000 men had already been withdrawn and now Nixon was promising that yet another 50,000 would be out by the spring of the year. Nor was there any guarantee it would stop there. Maybe Nixon had it in mind to change his image to Mister Nice-Guy?

Maybe it *was* time to quit?

Dempsey had had a good war. He'd made a lot of contacts and a lot of money. A fuck of a lot of very big people owed him a fuck of a lot of very big favours.

Maybe it was time to start calling his debts in ... start setting his sights on some top echelon Admin job that would inevitably lead to even greater things. A West Point posting would do to begin with; that was a time-honoured and smoothly-oiled gateway to the seat of ultimate power itself, the Pentagon. Certainly, West Point would do very nicely. Very nicely indeed.

If he could just clear his desk here, and bury the past— cover his tracks completely. No damn good getting out if in, say, five years' time a horde of little shits came a-knocking on his door, begging-bowls at the ready.

For the moment he had two prime and urgent objectives. One was to get Nguen Ton Chi off his back, and that meant finding another courier to head up north. The other was to cook Hardin's goose. Hardin could cause him a lot of trouble; he needed to be dealt with fast, but in as circumspect a manner as was humanly possible.

The contacts—what did he know; *who* did he know? He must have names, for Chrissake, and some of those names could result in a Goddamn shooting-party at dawn!

And the Tun Phouc business. Jesus, that was over a year ago; nearly two years, in fact. Merely the thought of what he'd done to cover that up caused sweat to break out on Dempsey's brow. Damn smart move to land Stocker with that good safe desk-job out of the way, and ...

'God-*damn!*'

Dempsey jerked himself forward and jabbed at a button

46

on his phone system.

'Yes, General?'

'Get me Sergeant Stocker.'

'Phone, General?'

'No. Here. *Fast!*'

Dempsey flicked off the intercom and relaxed back in his chair again. He reached for a cheroot, lit it, puffed smoke out in a long luxurious plume.

This would kill two birds with one stone, by God.

No—*three* birds with one stone! Hardin, Nguen Ton Chi—and Stocker, who'd always been something of a nagging worry at the back of his mind.

Dempsey glanced at his watch.

Where in hell was Alkine? Taking his crapping time, wasn't he? Sometime soon he'd have to make up his mind about Alkine: whether to take him along, or dump him. Alkine didn't know everything; didn't know about the hotel off Tu Do, for instance. On the other hand he'd been useful over the past few years, no doubt about that. It really all depended on how this operation went.

He turned to the next file.

'Happiness is a cold LZ!' joked Lieutenant Gafford, three seconds before a soft-nosed bullet struck him just below the left eye and, expanding rapidly as it drove through cranial bone, took away half the back of his head on its way out the other side.

Leroy Vogt, eyes wide, mouth open, hunkered down in a half-crouch slightly behind, thought: Oh my God, I can't handle this . . . *I can't!*—as Gafford, an expression of faint surprise on what was left of his face, started to topple backwards.

Vogt looked despairingly up at the choppers, tilting into the sky, the leaders already beginning to race away beyond the treeline, out of sight. A small Cobra 'Gunslinger' scout in the rear suddenly disappeared in a fat black explosion laced with orange streaks; bits of torn and twisted metal tumbled lazily down into the trees not 50 metres away.

Vogt watched them fall. Paradoxically, he was conscious of an overpowering desire to fly; just flap his arms and soar up into the cloudless blue of the sky. He'd surely be safe up there: a tiny dot not even a marksman could finger.

Ranged right across the grassy landing zone men were sprinting towards the trees, firing as they ran. A machine gun had opened up from the side of a small knoll and was raking the undergrowth in long chattering bursts. Someone was yelling 'Corpsman! Corpsman!', and Vogt watched as a black medic scuttled across his line of vision, his bags and packs bouncing on his back, his head ducking down every few seconds to inspect a body fleetingly, rather like a hen being chased by a fox but still stabbing its beak groundwards in a greedy search for grain. On an impulse, Vogt jabbed his rifle in the direction of Lieutenant Gafford's still form, and the corpsman ducked over it then bolted on again crying 'Fo'-*gayyt* it!'

Vogt thought: What the hell do I do? Run for the trees? Chances of me reaching them are about a zillion to one! God God God.

He felt very sick. His stomach was turning over and over,

his legs and arms felt weak, and despite the heat of the day his brow was icy-cold. He felt he couldn't have moved an inch from where he was if a VC had come right up to him and poked a gun in his face, and as he thought this a violent blow slammed into the small of his back and he tipped over on his face, gagging and retching as his mouth ground into the earth.

A hand grabbed the collar of his combat fatigues, tugged his head back violently.

'You little shit! Get your ass up outa here and *gallop* for those trees! *You hear me?*'

Vogt gave a faint cry and vomited what was left of his C-rat breakfast over the grass in front of him, a thick multihued stream of bile. He felt unbelievably wretched.

It had to be Sergeant Morelli. Morelli had been picking on him since he'd joined the squad a week ago. He'd done nothing right and it seemed like he never would do anything right, however hard he tried. Morelli had about used up his notoriously vast (Vogt had been told) stock of obscene epithets on him, and now here Morelli was, gazing down at him in the extremities of his misery. God God God.

Morelli was big and bulky and extravagantly Italianate. He had thick glossy black hair and an immense black moustache, curled up at the ends. He had very large hands, and those hands were now grasping Vogt by the lapels of his combat jacket as Morelli lifted him up off the ground and jammed his face down at him so they were almost nose to nose. Vogt desperately fought back the physical urge to be sick again. God, he'll *kill* me if I throw up all over his face!

Morelli hissed through film star's teeth: 'Goddamn it, Vogt—*you ... piss ... me ... off*! D'you hear what I say, Vogt? YEW ... PISS ... ME ... OFF! There's men fightin' and dyin' all around us, and all you can think of doin' is pukin' your rabbit's guts all over the fucking ground! You're useless, Vogt! Y'hear? YEW-SLESS! You're about as superfluous as a dribble of piss down a dog's hind legs! SOO-PER-FUCK-IN-FLOO-US!'

Morelli closed his mouth and glared at Vogt, and Vogt was suddenly aware that Morelli's eyes were brown and soft, not at all like a madman's eyes. He was also aware of a background sound tapestry of bangs and thuds and yells and hollers, and of the rock-solid fact that there seemed to be no one else within sight, not even the MG section, and that they must be a standing target, situated as they were in the middle of the empty landing zone, of quite unparalleled juiciness.

Morelli's muscles bulged as he lifted Vogt clear off the ground by a foot or more, shook him violently, then banged him down again and let him go. Vogt staggered, his arms automatically flapping for balance. Morelli shook his head slowly, almost uncomprehendingly.

'I really don't know why I bother with you fucking newts. I really don't.'

He grabbed Vogt's arm and pushed him down towards the ground.

'You stick right behind me, Vogt. Do everything I tell you. You stick to me like we was both dancin' fruits and you're butt-fuckin' me in the closet. *That close!*'

Morelli turned, unslung his rifle, and began to sprint towards the trees, dodging and weaving like a footballer heading for the line. Vogt followed at a shambling trot.

Just inside the trees Calhoun, a black two-striper from Illinois, was on his stomach beside a thorn bush pumping rounds at the other side of the grove where thick undergrowth stretched away to one side. Straight ahead, beyond the trees, rice paddies extended for maybe a half mile to another treeline.

'We got 'em, Sarge!' whooped Calhoun. 'The dimbos got 'emselves snared in the brush. They gonna haveta make a break 'cross the paddies. Fuckin' open season!'

Morelli grinned savagely and slung a grenade at the bushes. Vogt ducked his head automatically at the blast, squeezing his eyes tight shut as shards of wood blew along his bowed back. Opening his eyes again he saw that the grove was alive with figures, stooping, ducking, crouching, hugging the tiniest bump in the ground for cover, and blazing away at the tangle of undergrowth.

Vogt peered over the top of a gnarled clawlike tree-root, and fired at the bushes too. Not that he could see any movement there. How could *anything* move under that withering blast? There must be just *scores* of bodies piling up under the leaves during all this.

Bodies bodies bodies.

That's all it was. That's all he'd seen in the past week. Bodies. Lying everywhere, untended, unburied, heaped or single, sprawling in ungainly positions. The children were the worst. Oh God, the children, the little children. No legs, arms, no heads sometimes, gashed and torn, surrounded by ragged piles of viscera. No one had even *hinted* about the children.

What the hell am I doing here? thought Vogt, for the thousandth time. I should've dodged the draft; gone anywhere—Canada, South America, Sweden, even Cuba—but here. Others managed it; why in God's name couldn't I? God God God.

And everything happens so *fast* out here, he thought. It's unbelievable! And so arbitrary! When the choppers dropped them the LZ *was* what they called cold. There was no one to be seen for miles and miles. Not a hint of a movement. And then—bang! Just like that! Lieutenant Gafford gets his, and all hell breaks loose.

A sudden movement caught his eye.

'They runnin'!' yelled Calhoun.

Two, three, six, more than that—black-clad figures—hurtling out from the trees and across the paddies as though from a catapult.

Instantly lines of fire swerved, homed in on them, converged, caught them, seemed to throw them all into the air at once. The noise was indescribable, ear-pounding, pandemonic.

Morelli was bawling at Calhoun.

'Keep to the trees! They're still in there. Fuckin' bunker, you betcha! We'll flush 'em! Shift the assholes with *Ex-Lax*!'

He rose and started running. Vogt hard on his heels. Out of the corner of his eye he saw Calhoun yelling over his shoulder then following.

Morelli swerved away from the bushes and out of the trees, back on to the LZ. Stooped down, a massive figure still, he sprinted along a dyke then scrambled up and over the edge and plunged back into the grove again. He didn't seem to be breathing at all rapidly.

'Keep behind me, shitstick,' he muttered, squeezing

51

himself up alongside the bole of a tree. 'God damn! Those sneaky little yellow men. Y'know what, Vogt? We could lose this shitting war. Y'know why? 'Cos when did you last see a half-dozen grunts sacrificin' themselves for the good of the shitting cause? That's why we just might be on the fucking losing side, craphound.'

Vogt screwed his face up in perplexity.

'I don't get what you're saying, Sergeant. I really don't.'

'You *piss-ball*!' hissed Morelli ferociously. 'There's a bunker in there. *Right?* There's maybe two dozen gooners in the bunker. *Right?* We got the bunker surrounded. *Right?* So they send out a half-dozen men, knowin' full fucking well that we'll blow 'em away. *Right?*' With every '*Right?*' Morelli jabbed a finger hard into Vogt's chest, as though he was trying to drill his way through to the other side. 'So while we're whoopin' it up and tellin' ourselves what great fucking shots we are, them that's left in the bunker sneak out and nail our nuts. *Right?*' He suddenly grinned, and it seemed to Vogt that the grin was actually human, devoid of any trace of rage or hatred.

'Jesus Christ, Vogt, I seen a thousand like you, an' two-thirds of 'em we shipped back to the World in body-bags. You got a year out here, whether you like it or not. Most of you don't, but you gotta fucking hack it, is all. You just gotta eat shit to survive.'

Morelli started to turn away.

'So c'mon, smackhead—let's us *get some*!'

And that was when things suddenly went straight down the tube, very very fast.

Vogt said, 'Oh Christ!'

Coming towards them, through the trees, was a child. A little girl. Seven, maybe eight. Her face and arms were streaked with mud. Her thin cotton dress was torn right across the front, exposing her smooth golden belly and tiny half-formed pudenda. She was crying: clutching to her a fat raggedy-doll made of straw, with ludicrously large black-button eyes. She ran towards them, her mouth open, wailing with fright and terror, her arms lifting beseechingly, the doll extended in her tiny clutching hands.

Morelli snarled, '*Shit!*' and pulled his M-16 round at her.

To Vogt it was as though a film had stopped running on a screen in front of his eyes. The scene was frozen—a scene out of some kind of gross pornographic movie that was only to be seen in the rankest of Times Square houses, that you only heard about vaguely, that you never saw yourself. Except, it seemed, in real life.

The film jerked into motion again and Morelli was thrusting his M-16 right at the girl, and Vogt shrieked 'No, Sarge!' even as he pulled up his own rifle and sent a long burst hammering into the big man.

Blood exploded out of Morelli's back in long spurting streaks. He was like someone who was being electrocuted, as Vogt's rounds tore into his flesh, jolting him across the clearing in a spasmodic, stumbling, drunken dance. He let out a long wailing scream as the pounding impact finally smashed his equilibrium and punched him over on his face.

And even as that happened Vogt caught a sudden horrifying glimpse of a dimpled smirk on the little girl's face—before that too, as in a film, dissolved ... disappeared in a cloudy spray of blood and bone.

Even as he realised that someone behind him was firing he saw the doll fly out of the little girl's tiny hands and sail across the clearing to bounce against a tree trunk. He caught sight of something round and black and shiny drop from the straw on impact, and then what felt like a runaway steer slammed into the back of his legs, pitching him over.

'Down!' howled Calhoun.

The explosion seconds later, blew the tree away and cleared most of the brush for yards around.

Numbly, Vogt staggered to his feet. His head was buzzing and ringing and he felt he was going to be sick again. His rifle was on the ground, but he couldn't pick it up, his hands were shaking too much. He leaned against a tree and gaped at the scene, trying and failing to take in what he could see with his eyes; trying and failing to rationalise the experience.

Sergeant Morelli lay at his feet, his head twisted back at an odd angle, his soft brown eyes staring glassily at nothing.

Calhoun, carrying his Armalite, padded into sight, past Vogt and towards the little girl. He kicked her body viciously.

'Muth'fuckers,' he said.

He turned to Vogt, his black face streaked with sweat, his eyes bulging angrily.

'Shee-it, Vogt. The mud on her dress, Dig? I mean, doan you know? She in the *bunker*! They send her out, man! She give you one big ole pretty-please smile, then blow yo' balls off. Doan you *know*?'

Vogt stared down at the bloody mess that had once been Sergeant Morelli in stunned bewilderment.

'Ole Sarge, heah,' continued Calhoun, *'he* know. But Jesus, you jus' blow him away. Man,' he shook his head slowly, 'you in *bi-iiig* trouble!'

*   *   *

Captain Alkine picked up the phone, made sure it was secure, and said, 'Luke.'

The voice at the other end said, 'We have your boy, Vern. The name's Jesse Hardin. Works on the Rochester Telegram-Enquirer.'

'That was quick.'

'So happened we had a file on him. He's been making himself very snotty. Peace rallies and such. It wasn't very difficult.'

'You're sure he's the right one?'

'Sure I'm sure, Vern. Ain't two guys of that name who have ranking kin in Special Forces. Why we had a file on him in the first place.' Dowling paused. 'So?'

Alkine was in his own room. Like Dempsey, he was rarely there. What with one thing and another, he was often far too busy to attend to the work for which he was paid by the Army. The office was smaller than Dempsey's and, if anything, even more sparsely furnished. The one main difference was the Venetian blinds that hung, closed over the two windows. Alkine never opened them. He'd forgotten what the view looked like outside, and didn't particularly care if he was never reminded of it again. He felt safer with the blinds tightly closed.

'So?' repeated Dowling.

'Sorry, Luke. Yes, the boy. Newspaperman. Well, it seems to me you're going to have to cancel his subscription.'

'It seems,' said Dowling, 'to *you*?'

'Well, I think that would be the general opinion around here, Luke. Yes, I really do.'

'The *general* opinion?'

'Almost certainly.'

'*Almost*? For Christ's sake, Vern!'

'Let's just do it, Luke, okay? Just cancel. Seeing as how you have a file on him anyhow, it'll be a load off all our minds.'

There was silence from Dowling's end of the line.

'Luke?' said Alkine.

'Well, okay, Vern. But you better tell the man he's running out of favours.'

Alkine made a thin snorting noise through his nose. It was, for him, the equivalent of a loud belly-laugh.

'Well, I'll tell him, Luke, sure. But I think we still have a few left in the bag. All things considered. I really do.'

Alkine put the phone down. Suddenly, he was worried. He'd been keeping, he knew, a tight rein on Dempsey's affairs, and this was by no means the first time a wipe-out had been ordered. But he had a sudden gut-feeling that events were getting out of control; that he was reaching a stage where he'd no longer be able to handle them. That thought was almost frightening. He brushed it aside in his mind, tried to bury it under an avalanche of schemes and ideas and images—but it refused to stay buried.

It had nothing to do with Hardin's cousin or even Hardin himself. Not directly. But they were all a part of something larger, infinitely more threatening.

The odd hint here; the odd rumour there. A hell of a lot of people had it in for Dempsey, even though they could do nothing about him directly. They were either too scared, or simply too much in debt in one way or another. But still there were a *hell* of a lot of guys who would, given the chance, be only too delighted to reach for their knives and lunge for Dempsey's midriff.

Alkine stripped paper off a slice of gum, popped the gum

into his mouth, and began to chew.

This Hardin business: strictly a sideshow. Tie Hardin up somehow; knock off his cousin, just in case: small potatoes. They'd go away. Dempsey's main problem was Nguen Ton Chi, and he most definitely wouldn't. Not until Dempsey paid off *his* debts. And even then—well, Chi was a wily character. Hell, he had to be, in his position! A powerful and respected member of the South Vietnamese government, he had to keep up appearances. Dempsey had thought it had been a smart move eliciting aid from that quarter when an operation had begun to get a little hot, and it had paid off. No question about that. Nguen Ton Chi had been most accommodating, even when he'd presented the final bill. And what a bill. Alkine didn't like to think about it. He'd been associated with some dark operations before now, but this—Hell, this was something else again.

And now that Dempsey was about to get himself out of pawn . . . was about to clear the debt . . . Alkine wondered if it had ever occurred to him that Chi might come back for more; might not be entirely satisfied with payment, high as it was.

Alkine had the sudden feeling that he was on the edge of a whirlpool; not yet spiralling down into the treacherous funnel of darkness that seemed to beckon to him almost hypnotically, but spinning nearer and nearer, almost there, his struggles becoming more and more futile as he hurtled round. *Out of control!*

He went out of his office and walked slowly back down to Dempsey's. Dempsey looked up as he came in.

'Dowling?' he grunted.

'All seen to, General. Everything is tight.'

Dempsey opened his mouth as though to say something else, then shook his head. He reached for another file from the thinning pile and gestured at the chair in front of his desk.

'Siddown,' he said, and opened out the file.

PEPPER

Doc Pepper took another hit of the fat brown-paper joint and made *tyip-tyip-tyip* noises with his lips as he sucked smoke deep. His eyes crossed delicately.

Sanger said, 'Hoo-*ee*! Ole Doctor Pepper is im-*bi*-bing on his fuh-*ay*-verit con-*cock*-shun!' and rolled over on the mattress, cackling like a mad scientist.

Doc Pepper smiled; chuckled quietly. He eased himself back against the wall and sighed contentedly. The muscles just above his knees were beginning to tingle, his eye-lids felt heavy, and he had an idea that his nose didn't belong to him.

'Come on,' said the English photographer, 'pass it along. What you don't seem to realise, you Yankees, is that smoking dope is strictly a social habit.'

'Peace and love!' snorted Sanger, hugging his stomach. 'Peas an' *lu-uuuhv*!'

Doc Pepper passed it on. The Englishman took a couple of quick drags then held the joint up at an angle, staring at it with a slight frown on his untanned face.

'The way I do it,' he said, 'is the correct way. I mean, it lasts longer, for Heaven's sake. The way our medical friend here does it you'd think he was trying to get smashed out of his mind in the quickest manner possible.' He turned to Doc Pepper. 'Isn't that so?'

Doc Pepper said, 'What?'

The Englishman said, 'That. Isn't that so?'

Doc Pepper said, 'Isn't what so, man?'

The Englishman frowned some more, gazing at a spot just about one o'clock high of the top of Doc Pepper's head.

'I'm not too sure,' he said thoughtfully. 'What was I saying?'

Doc Pepper chuckled again, wriggling slightly so he could feel his shoulder-blades gently grinding into the plaster of the wall. He yawned.

'That's it!' said the Englishman, snapping his fingers, and dropping the joint down the front of his pants. He was sitting cross-legged on the mattress, and he muttered strange curses as he dug around with his fingers trying to find it.

'Burn your balls off, man!' giggled Sanger, rolling off the mattress on to the floor. 'That's what you're gonna *do-ooo*!'

The Englishman rescued the joint and firmed it out, taking another couple of quick drags.

'You of all people in this room,' he went on, pointing accusingly at Doc Pepper, 'should know that the deeper you suck the quicker it gets into the bloodstream. I mean, this is an established medical fact. There is no denying it. I have yet to hear someone tell I'm a liar with regard to this.' He paused, glancing up towards the ceiling which was peeling and dirty. A small lizard clung to the wall high up, defying gravity.

Doc Pepper nodded.

'Well, I'll tell you, man,' he said, stretching lazily, 'that's exactly why I do it like I do it. Exactly.'

'Eggs-*ackly*!' hooted Sanger. '*Eeeegs*-ackly!'

In the corner by the door Schofield, the American photographer, was assembling his needle, preparatory to hooding up. It was a brand new needle and he fitted it together with practised ease, smiling all the while. He was a tall, well-proportioned man, as opposed to the English photog who was short and stocky. The Englishman had the makings of a moustache on his upper lip; Schofield's was thick and black and slightly shiny. Schofield fiddled with his bits of plastic and steel, and licked his lips in dreamy anticipation.

'Man, man, man,' he said, deep-voiced, 'I dunno what it is with you, Doc. You wanna slow down time, I wanna speed it up; make the days go bip-bip-bip.'

'*Speed* it up,' said Sanger, chuckling as though at a rather clever and amusing story.

'Get by the grey times,' Schofield went on, reaching for his ivory box. 'Get 'em outta the way damn fast.'

'S'evil stuff, you know that, man?' said Doc Pepper. 'You know that is really bad shit. I can tell you things. Things I've seen, man. I can really tell you things. But,' he gave a snorting giggle, 'I don't want to.'

Schofield looked up.

'What d'you mean, bad shit? You speaking figuratively?

58

Generally? Or d'you mean *this* is bad shit?'

'No, man, I mean *all* that needle shit is bad shit. Hooked-up shit, is what I mean.'

A memory trembled on the edge of Doc Pepper's mind.

Schofield had said, 'Make it prime now, Doctor Pepper,' wagging a finger, 'none of that Number Ten shit, right? Boo-coo good!' And Goddamnit, he'd forgotten to pick the stuff up off Cresswell, he'd been in such a hurry to get off Base. Luckily, he'd spotted a contact in Tu Do, the joker who ran all those 12-year-old girls fat redneck juicer NCOs seemed to go for. The contact was not a very nice man, and Doc Pepper tended to avoid him if he could; but he was useful, there was no getting away from that. And no time more than right now, with him late and Schofield tapping his fingers down to the cuticles in his room at the Royal Hotel. Naturally, the contact had some on him—*naturally!*—and naturally he'd urged Doc Pepper to try—just try—one of the girls, just seen peeping out of an alley with an already professional smile curving her lips and her big dark eyes pools of fuzzed bewilderment. Just as naturally Doc Pepper had shaken his head—'No, no, no; not my scene, man!'—even as the contact pointed out that this one was really Number One, 'very pliable', (and where in hell had he picked *that* up?), 'very good after shot', and Doc Pepper had muttered 'It isn't for *me*, man!', and he paid his green, grabbed the bag, and run.

None of this surfaced at all in concrete images now; just quick flashes in his mind, that made no sense. And it was too difficult to link them all up and tell the story. Sure it was good shit. Hell, the contact wouldn't fuck him about. Would he?

'No, man. It's just *all* bad shit, is what it is. Sometimes I don't understand you, Schofield, bright guy like . . .'

Doc Pepper's voice drifted to a standstill, and he yawned.

Schofield said, 'Heaven will take care of its own.' He was carefully spooning the powder into a tiny ladle, measuring by eye. He got up, stretched, and walked over to the sink.

'Jesus, one of these days I'm gonna tell that fucking Corsican what I think of his fucking hotel,' he grumbled, staring down at the cracked and filthy porcelain. 'It is a shithole.'

'It's your room,' the Englishman pointed out. 'You keep it clean.'

'That is the sort of smug, moralistic, self-satisfied and sententious remark I would've expected from you, old boy,' said Schofield, who'd majored in English and wrote his own copy.

'Sorry, I'm sure,' muttered the Englishman. He passed the joint down to Sanger who was now lying full-length on the floor, humming to himself.

'Wheee!' whinneyed Sanger. 'Another hit!'

Doc Pepper yawned again, easing himself off the wall and into a cross-legged position.

'Knock off the bad vibes, Schofield,' he said. 'I have enough of that shit out in the fuckin' bush. I mean, I came here to relax, not hear a bunch of bad-mouthers throwin' words at each other.'

He sighed, and it was almost as though this action flipped a switch in his mind, turning on his internal TV set. As he gazed at nothing outwardly, inwardly the images, previously blurred and undefined, sharpened up. He was back *out there*, and there was plasma, field dressings ('Put Other Side Next To Wound'), bandages, needles, pills, ampules, and lots and lots of rounds, all, seemingly, ranged in on him as he sprinted this way and that like a dog with his tail on fire.

'You out there again?' said Schofield sympathetically.

'It's no shit. I am truly *out there*.'

'Charlie really digs medics,' said Schofield to the Englishman.

'Oh?'

'Yeah. Hit a medic a day, it'll pay your way, in the NVA.' Schofield took a glass dropper from his makings, ran it under the cold tap. 'They got a little game—hit point-man, but not to kill him. That's so he'll scream, and they can take out the medic when he comes a-running. Smart move.'

'Barbarians,' sniggered Sanger, cupping the joint.

'Sure,' agreed Schofield. 'Same like us.'

'Tell me,' said the Englishman, 'do the Americans really—you know, collect things out there? You know— *ears*, and things? Cut them off? Souvenirs?'

'Oh, man!' Doc Pepper sank back against the wall, a pained expression on his face. 'Knock it off, will you. Gimme the joint, Sanger. I am beginning to feel them old dark clouds rolling over me. Je-sus!'

Schofield had run water into a glass and was now using the dropper to suck it up and drip it into the ladle.

'No dark clouds with this sweet grain, my boy,' he said. 'Take it from one who knows.'

'Someone else who knows,' whispered Sanger. He reached up, clutched at the Englishman's right knee and shook it. 'Tell me, Mr Englishman, who knows what evil lurks in the heart of man?' His voice became throaty, urgent. 'Tell me, tell me!'

'What evil? What? I don't know.'

'I'll tell you who knows, my friend.' Sanger's voice curved up to a croaked and rasping peak. 'The *Shadow* knows! *The Sha-dow knows!*' He spun round on his back and sat up, pointing both hands at the Englishman as though they were guns. '*Bam-bam-bam!*' His voice went down again to a hoarse whisper. 'Two .45 automatics have just cleaned the evil outta your soul, Mr Englishman.' He flopped back on to the floor again, laughing wildly.

Doc Pepper rubbed his eyes and chuckled softly. Sanger was really an outrageous sonuvabitch. Goddamnit, he was.

'You're a sonuvabitch, Sanger. You're a sonuvabitch now, you've been a sonuvabitch all the time I've known you, and you'll be a sonuvabitch till the day you die. A really outrageous sonuvabitch.'

'Out-*rage*-uz!' howled Sanger, drumming his heels on the floor.

'Cut it out, Sanger,' said Schofield from the sink. 'You'll put the hoodoo on us, for Christ's sake.'

'Hoo-doo?' murmured Sanger. 'I do! D'do-ron-ron, is what I d'do-hoo-hoo!'

Holding his ladle carefully in one hand and the water glass in the other, Schofield walked back to his corner and sat down on the bed. He reached for some cotton balls and a bottle of surgical spirit and placed them on the bedside table.

'Lighter,' he said to the Englishman.

The Englishman tossed him the Zippo, and Schofield caught it one-handed.

'Home cooking,' he said. 'You wanna try some?'

The Englishman shook his head.

'To tell you the truth, I can't stand needles.'

'You wanna snort then, but this way's quicker. Oh so quicker.'

'Even so,' said the Englishman primly.

'Wise man,' said Doc Pepper, taking another hit. 'Them old mainline junkies are evil dudes with evil ways. They'll take you down the primrose fucking path to your doom. It's all the US army's fault.'

'I don't think I caught the jump,' said the Englishman.

'I don't think there was one,' said Doc Pepper.

'He means,' said Schofield, letting the lighter flame gently caress the bottom of the ladle, 'that if the authorities hadn't suddenly decided to blow the whistle on what used to be called, rather charmingly I always thought, Sweet Mary J, the guys over here would still all be rampaging around in their reckless reefer ravings. As it is, they're all shooting up like there's no tomorrow. Which, in many cases, there isn't.' He chuckled, watching the liquefaction process intently, gauging its readiness. 'A great notion. Simpler to carry, doesn't stink up the place, and treats you like a lady. Like a Goddamn lady.'

'Bad shit,' mumbled Doc Pepper.

Quite suddenly he was utterly depressed. In another week he'd be *out there* again, the cynosure of all rifle muzzles. He passed what remained of the joint to the Englishman and watched as Schofield loaded up. Schofield tied a damp cotton scarf round his upper arm, tugging on the knot with his teeth. The big vein bulged, and he rubbed it up even more. He shook the bottle of surgical spirit, uncapped it, placed a cotton ball over the mouth and upended. Then he swabbed the stuff over the vein. He smiled and said, 'I do the nicest things to myself,' and shot up.

'Oh my God,' quavered the Englishman.

He said this because Schofield's head suddenly jerked back and he gasped '*Ungh!*' explosively at the same time. His face was twisted up into a death's-head rictus of shock and agony.

'Oh, Christ, Oh Christ,' said Doc Pepper, trying to get to his feet so fast that he slipped and fell over on to his face.

Schofield, the needle still in his arm, gave a thin scream and rolled sideways off the bed, knocking into the bedside table and sending his makings clattering to the floor. He landed on his needle-arm atop the water glass, which shattered. Shards of glass sank into the exposed flesh and the vein and quite suddenly there was blood all over the place and Schofield was heaving around on the floor like a landed fish, his face as white as the driven snow and his eyes wide and staring.

'Oh my God,' mumbled the Englishman.

'*The scarf!*' screamed Doc Pepper.

'Oh no,' whispered Sanger, hypnotised by the blood pumping out like a gusher. 'Oh crap.' He put his hands up to his face, uttered a low moan, and fainted.

At that moment the door crashed inwards with an appalling splintering sound and three MPs jumped into the room.

'You fuckers have had it!' snapped one.

The Englishman turned to them dazedly.

'No, listen. I'm accredited. I'm an accredited photographer with a British newspaper.'

'You say another word, shitface,' said the MP, 'and I'll tear your dick off and stuff it up your nose.'

Doc Pepper, tears streaming down his face, was crawling across the floor towards the twitching figure of Schofield. The MP surveyed the scene coldly, then put out one gloved hand and took hold of a good fistful of the Englishman's curly hair, tightening his grip, twisting the Englishman's head down towards his own.

'You fuckers have *had it!*' he hissed.

*   *   *

'I guess this one's the corpsman,' said Dempsey.

'It seemed to me, General, that such a squad as you seemed to have in mind ought to contain a medic of some description,' said Alkine.

'Neat, Alkine. Very crapping neat. No loose ends, huh?'

'I hope not, sir.'

'So do I, Alkine. So do I.'

Dempsey pushed the file to one side and selected another.

'You don't follow the horses, do you, Alkine?' he said.

Alkine shook his head.

'No, sir.'

'Selection, Alkine, is the name of the game. But we're not picking the winners, we're choosing the losers.' Dempsey let out a throaty guffaw. 'Choosing the crapping losers is what we're doing. You think this mission has the possibility of a high-success rating?'

'Frankly, General, I'm not too sure.'

Dempsey looked up, sudden anger darkening his face. He got to his feet and leaned across the desk, staring down at Alkine with the intensity of someone who has been in a madhouse for twenty years.

'Not too sure is shit, Alkine,' he said through his teeth. 'Not too sure is not a phrase I want to hear from you, no way. You just wind that gnat's brain of yours up to positive, you hear what I say? Anything on this operation fouls up and your balls'll get minced up and thrown to the dogs so fast you won't know it's Christmas. You understand me?'

Alkine nodded. It was pointless to remind Dempsey that he hadn't been given details of the actual operation as yet. When you were in Dempsey's pocket you learned to roll with the punches.

'I certainly do, General.'

Dempsey's chair creaked as he sat back in it, still glowering at his subordinate. Then he glanced at his watch.

'Stocker's taking his damn time,' he muttered.

'*Stocker?*'

For once, Alkine's voice pitched high. For a moment he could hardly believe he'd heard right. Could the General actually have mentioned Stocker? He stared at Dempsey open-eyed, and felt a twinge—but no more than that; he'd disciplined himself too well over the years—of panic touch him.

'Sure, Stocker. So?'

'My God, General, the man's a psychopath.'

Dempsey's lips lifted briefly in a bleak smile.

'Kind of an exaggeration, wouldn't you say, Captain?'

'No, sir. With all respect, I'd have to say that might be putting it damn mildly.'

'You could be right, Alkine. But it seems to me I couldn't have chosen a better man for the job I have in mind. Loyal, got guts, straight in to his target and no pussy-footing around. Correct me if I'm wrong, Alkine, but that's the kind of character who'll prove invaluable on an operation like this.'

Alkine didn't say anything, so Dempsey started to read the penultimate file.

'Sure,' said Garrett. 'Easy as falling off a log. No problem at all. You just name a time and place, and if the price is right, your man is dead.'

He was a solid-looking man; had the build of a heavyweight not yet gone to seed. Maybe in a year or two he would start running to fat if he didn't look after himself, but for now he was in good condition, and he knew it. He could out-handwrestle anyone on the Base, and off it.

From a distance, and if he happened to be smiling (a rare occurrence), he looked like a regular Joe, one of the guys, a man you could split a quart of rye with and no harm done. It was only when you got up close that you saw the hooded eyes, ever watchful, alive with suspicion, and the thin bloodless lips, pursed in such a way that you realised he always kept his teeth tight together in his mouth. A bad sign.

Now he passed his right hand back over his close-cropped reddish hair and smiled with his thin lips as fast as a camera shutter clicking.

'So let's nail the price right down,' he said.

The man opposite him in the bar-booth was a Vietnamese businessman named Ngo Van Toan. He was dressed in a neat dark suit, and he wore round-lensed glasses. His skin was sallow and unlined, except for two small pouches under his eyes, and it was difficult to guess his age. Not that Garrett was all that interested in guessing the slope's age. Forty, fifty, who cared? As long as his roll was good, that was all that mattered. Whatever it was, however, he looked very much out of place in the bar, and every so often he would wince at the rock music blaring out of the hidden loudspeakers.

'But before we do that let's us have another little drink,' said Garrett.

He nodded to one of the bored-looking, mini-skirted, seethrough-bloused girls at the other end of the nearly empty room. The girl wandered over with a tray: beer for Garrett, iced water for Ngo Van Toan.

She put the tray down and looked at Garrett then at the Vietnamese. Neither made a move. The girl gave a not so delicate snort, surveyed the room from end to end, then tapped a heel on the floor.

'Drinks,' she said, and made to take the tray up again. Garrett put out a hand and prised her fingers off the tray.

'The money,' said Garrett.

The Vietnamese winced and drew out a wallet from an inner front pocket of his pants. He paid.

'You no want business with him,' the girl said to Garrett. 'I give you business, big boy. Plenty business. Number One business. You like very much.'

'Get the fuck out of here, bitch,' said Garrett, not even looking at her. The girl wandered off.

'I would say that three thousand would be a good price.' said Garrett.

Ngo Van Toan raised his eyebrows nervously.

'That is a lot of piastres.'

This time Garrett flashed his teeth.

'That's dollars, pal. Greenies. I can get all the toilet paper I want back at Base.'

The Vietnamese nodded seriously, as though Garrett had just uttered a cosmic truth.

'Yes. That is correct. But you will do this. Very important. This man very evil. A very bad man. Threaten my business.'

'Sure, sure. But I need an advance. I'll take a third now.'

Ngo Van Toan stared down at the table, sipped at his iced water, then shook his head.

'No. One-sixth. Five hundred dollars.'

'Forget it,' said Garrett, beginning to get angry.

The Vietnamese shrugged; got up. As he did this, Garrett ran throuh in his mind his more urgent personal debts and thought: The hell with it. He could always shake the wimpy little fucker down for more afterwards.

'Okay, okay. Put it on the table. Tell me where and when.'

The Vietnamese dived into another pocket and placed an envelope on the table. They discussed time and place, and other matters germane to the transaction. Garrett yawned.

'You only common soldier,' said the Vietnamese

suddenly. 'Not officer.'

'That's no lie.'

'I thought you more than common soldier. I thought you corporal.'

'That was months ago. They keep on busting me up and down like a Goddamn yo-yo.'

'Busting?'

'Yeah. I'm a real badass. I take no shit. So the cocksuckers bust me.'

'Ah! Cocksucker!' Ngo Van Toan smiled a knowing and enthusiastic smile. 'You a cocksucker?'

'Jesus Christ,' muttered Garrett. He took a long pull at his beer and thought about the money.

'But you able to get around?' said the Vietnamese urgently. 'Some places off-limits. I know this.'

'I can get around,' said Garrett, which was true. 'You got an angle, you can get around.'

'Tomorrow?'

'Sure, sure. He's already croaked. Don't panic.'

He watched the man disappear in the jostling crowd of Marines that had just entered the bar. The girls at the other end of the room all began to smile and laugh and chatter animatedly amongst themselves, casting roguish glances at the oncoming horde, as though someone had just thrown a switch back-stage. The Marines whistled and made gestures and talked dirty in loud whispers. Garrett got to his feet.

He nodded to a fellow he knew, and the fellow lifted an eyebrow in comic shock.

'Say, man, what the hell you doing with the dink? He's a mean mother, take it from me.'

'So am I,' said Garrett, pushing his way towards the door.

'No, man, I mean he's a *mean* mother. I know him. I mean, he's like a fucking *miser*, man.'

But Garrett was already out of earshot, heading into the street.

He thought about the situation that night and all the next morning. A fast hit. In and out, the way he liked it. And he thought about the money. The number lived on Pasteur, and that was Fat City. There was real loot there—old

68

French villas, trees lining the boulevard: the number had to be loaded. So what was three thousand, for Chrissake? Chicken-feed. Five thousand, maybe. Six, seven. Maybe even more. This was a big hit. He sensed it. Three thousand was letting the slope off too lightly.

Sure, he'd never done it for more back in the World, but here it was different. Way different.

Carelli dropped him off in a jeep just past one o'clock. Carelli figured something was up, but he didn't want to know about it. Wise man. Garrett told him ten minutes, a dozen houses down, and don't hang around.

He stepped into the driveway and turned briefly to gaze at the wide avenue. A Mercedes hummed past on the other side, a couple of Hondas. It was quiet; sleepy-time—why the slope had suggested it—and all you could smell were the mingled fragrances of poincianas and bougainvillea. The garden was rich with colour; Garrett recognised roses, but not much else. He was reminded of the last Stateside hit he'd made, down in Atlantic City five years ago, just before he'd had to get the hell out fast and join the army to escape those mad fuckers from Reno who wanted his head on a roasting dish. That number had been a flower-freak. Garrett had dealt with him in a large hot-house; a good place to die if you were a flower-freak.

Garrett was holding a briefcase, which looked businesslike but didn't mean a thing. He walked quickly up to the front door and pulled on the bell. When he heard footsteps the other side, he flipped open the briefcase and took out the .38, holding it so it was pointed at the door.

No maids at this hour, the Vietnamese had said, and no house-boys. You better have your facts right, Jim, thought Garrett.

An old man opened the door. *The* old man. He didn't look like an evil man at all, just very old. But you could never tell in this business. Garrett had known some very evil men who looked like Catholic priests—the sort of Catholic priests played by Barry Fitzgerald in late-show re-runs.

Garrett gestured with the gun and pushed the old man back inside. The old man began blabbering in Vietnamese; he was trembling and shaking and his eyes had filled with tears. The hallway was wide and cool, and Garrett pushed him backwards to the far end, reaching round him and opening a door which led to a dark passageway.

'This'll do,' he said, swivelling the old man round. 'Don't worry, pal. Won't take long.'

He kept the .38 hard in the old man's spine with his left hand, dropped the briefcase, and pulled the garotte out of his tunic pocket with his right. It consisted of four strands of piano wire twisted tightly together, each end fixed to a small but chunky wooden toggle.

'Fast and silent,' said Garrett conversationally.

He dropped the gun, and in one swift movement looped the wire over the old man's head down to his throat, cross-toggled and jerked smoothly outwards. The old man made a gulping noise for about half a second, and then the wire sliced through flesh and tissue and windpipe and beyond as though it was all butter, cutting the sound off, and nearly taking his head from his shoulders. Garrett unleashed the wire before the body became a dead weight and let the old man slip to the floor, his head slack and loose in a growing pool of blood.

Garrett cleaned the wire with a tissue and pocketed it. He checked there was no blood down the front of his uniform, then picked up the gun and the briefcase and began to walk across the hallway.

'Ten thousand,' he said. 'Professional.'

He checked his watch and opened the door. And froze.

Two Vietnamese policemen holding rifles filled the doorway, gazing at him with bleak expressions on their faces. Behind them was Ngo Van Toan, wringing his hands and shouting.

'That him! That him! Oh! Look! He kill my father!'

Having made his point in English, Ngo Van Toan lapsed into Vietnamese for the benefit of the two policemen.

'What is this?' yelled Garrett. 'You basstud! You never meant! You! This is a frame!'

He made to burst his way through, get at Ngo Van Toan, but one of the policemen thrust his rifle at his crotch and Garrett jack-knifed, screaming in agony. He didn't see the other cop smash the rifle-butt into his forehead. He only felt it.

'This crap sure as shit makes for compulsive reading, Alkine,' said Dempsey chattily, closing the Garrett file. 'Gripping. What d'you think of his story?'

Alkine was still thinking about Stocker, and the clear fact that Dempsey intended using him. The implications were terrifying. It surely meant that Dempsey's capacity for handling situations was breaking down; he was starting to wig out. This whole operation was fraught enough as it was, without an arbitrary factor like Stocker thrown into it. Stocker was a human time-bomb on a slow burn; who could say when he would detonate?

Suddenly aware that Dempsey had spoken, Alkine looked up, unusually muddy-minded.

'His story, General?'

'His crapping story, Alkine,' said Dempsey testily. 'Garrett's story, for Chrissake. He said he was set up by the slope. Set up to kill the slope's old man.'

Alkine lifted his hands.

'Who's to say, sir? Half of this crowd,' he indicated the files, 'could be telling the truth for all we know, but it makes no difference to what I guess you have in mind for them.'

Dempsey's jowls quivered as he let out a gusty laugh.

'Right! How Goddamn perceptive of you, Alkine! Not one blind duck's bit of difference! See, what I have in mind for these no-hopers is a rescue mission. Hell, if they bring it off they ought to get some kind of reward. Executive clemency, maybe. Yeah,' he chuckled, his voice dropping to a quieter, more confidential tone, as though he was seriously considering the idea, 'executive clemency, for services rendered above and beyond the, uh . . . call of duty. I like that, Alkine. I really like that.'

As you say, sir,' said Alkine, mentally calling upon his fairly vast reserves of patience. 'About . . . Stocker, sir . . .'

Dempsey looked up quickly, his eyes bleak.

'Forget Stocker,' was all he said, as he reached for the final file.

71

OLSEN

Staff Sergeant Walter Olsen was listening to Lieutenant Roger Durnaway.

The two men could hardly have been more different if one had been an Eskimo and the other an Australian aborigine. As it was Durnaway came from East Coast stock that stretched back to the 17th Century and was called Roger because every eldest Durnaway son had been called Roger since Christ was a teenager, and Olsen was from a Pennsylvanian mining family that stretched back to 1929 and was called Walter because he was the last in a large family and his mother had run out of names and then remembered she'd been taken to see Walter Huston in *Abraham Lincoln* on her first date with Olsen senior (a first generation Swede with an accent you could blunt an axe on, who hadn't understood one word that was said during the entire movie).

What with one thing and another, the two men did not see eye to eye on almost any subject you cared to mention, from cleaning an M-16 bolt with a toothbrush, through how to utilise C-ration cardboard to its fullest extent, right up to, say, the care and cultivation of Japanese dwarf pines. Not that Olsen thought about Japanese dwarf pines all that often, but he'd once heard a colonel or general or some brass like that jabbering away excitedly about them, and he remembered thinking that if the subject were to come up between him and Durnaway, whatever he said Durnaway'd shoot him down in flames with a few well-chosen words; make him feel a real numbnuts.

The fact was, Lieutenant Roger Durnaway was a prize asshole and A-1 shit. There was no getting away from that though Olsen would have liked to; he'd have liked to get away from this whole shooting war, but especially he'd like to be a few thousand miles from Durnaway.

Not, like now, standing a few feet from him and trying to avoid those icy blue eyes.

'What's the matter, Olsen? You can't look me straight in the eye? It makes you nervous, uncomfortable? Is that what it is?'

'No, sir,' muttered Olsen.

Durnaway shifted slightly in his seat.

'I'm having trouble hearing you, Sergeant.'

'I said, *nossir*,' said Olsen, raising his voice.

'I cannot hear what you say, Sergeant. And I cannot make up my mind whether this is due to the sloppy, mumbling way you speak, or it's some kind of insolence you're handing me.'

'NOSSIR!' shouted Olsen, his face brick-red, the veins standing out on his brow.

Durnaway nodded.

'Fine. Then when you come to see me, Olsen, you just look me straight in the eyes. That way we're on a man-to-man basis, which is exactly the way I like it.'

Durnaway pursed his lips thoughtfully, picked up a pencil from the crate that served as a table, and began to sharpen it with a small pocket-knife.

'Now,' he said, 'I think we'd better have a talkout, Sergeant. I believe there is something important we have to discuss.'

He said this in a cold, calm voice, and this was the way Lieutenant Roger Durnaway usually handled platoon business. There was nothing friendly or confiding about him, he was not a gregarious man. Fact was, he hated his grunts with a hatred that was only barely concealed. Nor was there anything racial about this. Durnaway loathed them all, whatever their colour, creed or ancestral nationality.

'Isaacs,' said Durnaway bleakly.

Talkout, thought Olsen, just as bleakly.

Why did Durnaway use that word? It had always puzzled him. It was a kind of a made-up word, absolutely the only one he used. And it didn't square with Durnaway's normal mode of speech at all, which, to give the mother-fucker his due, was clear and sharp and precise. There was no possibility of misunderstanding what Durnaway said about any subject under the sun; there were no ambiguous shades of meaning.

Except here. Far as Olsen could determine, 'talkout' ought to mean two guys chewing the fat together, arguing with each other, opinionating, trying to reach a conclusion via a mutual dismembering of a given subject. That was not how Durnaway saw its meaning. He stood you there and blasted you with words, and that was that. It was all very strange.

But then Durnaway was a strange man altogether. He didn't smoke, didn't drink, didn't use bad language, didn't laugh. Probably didn't screw either, man or woman. All in all he was Goddamn Martian.

'For some unknown reason,' Durnaway said, chipping away at the pencil, 'at least, Sergeant, unknown to me, Isaacs was amongst a party digging slit-trenches when I last saw him, not ten minutes ago. This surprised me, as I was under the impression I told you to put him out front in the Listening Post for the night.'

The canvas roof of the tent shuddered and then cracked viciously as a breeze from outside caught it. Olsen smelt rain.

He'd been out in Vietnam long enough to be able to gauge with some accuracy the state of the weather an hour or so into the future. It was no big deal. Lots of guys could do it, especially the country boys, but Olsen was proud of this minor feat because he'd been brought up in Pittsburgh and the only thing you could smell there was iron and steel and coke and dirt. It was one of the principal reasons he'd joined the army: to get away from Pittsburgh and all that crap laying heavy in the air.

Olsen had joined up a couple of years after Korea. His father had been dubious; couldn't see any merit in the army at all. Educational, social, career, or anything else. Especially after Korea, which no one seemed to have won, least of all his adopted country. Well, they said it was a victory, but Olsen senior wasn't so sure. He liked his wars cut and dried, and it seemed to him the Reds had got what they'd wanted in the first place: a slice of territory. That was losing?

None of this made any impression on Olsen junior, who went right ahead and joined up with enthusiasm. That enthusiasm took him through 14 years of shit and sweat; right up until six months ago, in fact, when he'd arrived in Nam for a second tour. That was when he began to have doubts.

Originally, as far as Olsen could see, they were in South Vietnam to stop the guys from North Vietnam taking over. On the surface, that seemed simple enough. Clear-cut. But was it?

Now, Olsen simply didn't know. From being stark black-and-white, the overall canvas of the conflict, as seen in his mind, began to dissolve—to run—into a wash of different, and subtle, shades of grey.

Trust was the main problem. Olsen liked the Vietnamese, on the whole. They seemed like a happy, friendly people, grateful for what Olsen and his buddies were doing for them. They trusted you to do the right thing, and, naturally, you trusted them in return to back you all the way. Right up to the hilt.

Now it was different. Now they didn't smile at you as you went past the rice paddies, didn't offer you presents, didn't chatter excitedly. They tried not to look at you now, or if you did happen to catch their eyes you saw blank pools in expressionless faces And you couldn't trust them—Jesus Christ, you simply *couldn't*—because you just did not know if the guy you were looking at was looking at you that way because he was dispirited and wished like hell for the shit to stop flying, or because come nightfall he'd be mortaring your perimeters and he couldn't wait to start.

The men were different, too. The grunts. They couldn't give a damn about anything any more: clothes, guns, officers, discipline. They just wanted to get the fuck back to the World, and Goddamnit, who could blame them? This fucking conflict was stripped sour—murderous, agonising, ultimately unwinnable. That was how it seemed to Olsen.

And to pile on shit, he was stuck with a crock of crap like Lieutenant Roger Durnaway, who hated his men; had absolutely no feeling for them, or understanding of them as human beings whatsoever.

'I'm waiting, Sergeant, for some sort of vocal response to my previous comments.' Durnaway put the pencil down on the crate-top and selected another. 'An explanation of the situation, Sergeant. Try very hard to be lucid, Sergeant, when you give it to me.'

Behind his back Olsen was knotting and clenching his

hands together. With great difficulty he stopped himself from jumping forward and taking a swing at Lieutenant Roger Durnaway, prize asshole and A-1 shit—the guy who so little understood what was going on out here that he'd seen Neff throw down a gum-wrapper in the hootch area, told him to pick it up and then when Neff had gaped tiredly and stupidly at him and said, 'Aw, c'mon, Loot!' had written him up. Neff, who'd only a half-hour before come back from the heaviest night patrol that week: eight men KIA, a passel of walking wounded and mucho panic-sweat. Written him up. For a Goddamn gum-wrapper.

Durnaway really got off on writing guys up. It was part of his charm. Often the sonuvabitch would sneak round the lines at night and catch a solid bag: guys listening to the radio, guys smoking, guys taking a quick catnap. All actions, it was true, against which disciplinary measures were taken back in the World. But, Jesus, this was Vietnam! This was hell on earth!

'Well, Isaacs, sir. He's got problems. I mean, I think I mentioned to you before, sir, he talks to himself in a kind of a crazy way. It's since his great-aunt died, sir, like I think I said.'

'You think, Sergeant?' asked Durnaway. 'I don't think you think at all. In fact, Sergeant, I'm certain of it. I'm well aware this distant member of his family died. I recall quite clearly you informing me of that fact. What I fail to understand is why you should believe, as you clearly do, that it makes any difference at all to my original order.'

'Well, sir, Isaacs was close to the old lady, sir, is what I heard. Had no other kin. He was kind of reared by her, sir.'

Durnaway's mouth twisted up and down briefly, as though he was trying to suck a morsel of meat from between his teeth and didn't want anyone to see him doing it.

'If I say Isaacs goes out on the Listening Post, Sergeant,' he said in a low voice, 'he goes out on the Listening Post.'

'Well, hell, sir, I really don't think it's right, sir. I have a strong feeling, sir, that the poor fucker is gonna do something . . . well, kind of stupid, sir.' Like blowing his Goddamn brains out, Olsen thought. 'He's been talking very wildly, sir. Frankly, sir, I think he needs to see

76

the . . .'

Durnaway's eyes closed, then opened again.

'*Get him out there, Sergeant.*'

Without saluting or speaking, Olsen turned on his heels and shambled towards the tent-opening. He went out into the gathering darkness. Yep, smelled like rain, sure enough. Another ten minutes, and *Pow!*—down'd come the wet stuff. Olsen wrinkled his nose. The thought of rain on his upturned face gave him real pleasure. He looked forward to it.

From back in the tent Lieutenant Roger Durnaway yelled, '*Sergeant!*'

Olsen took out the smooth, egg-shaped fragmentation grenade and smiled at it. This would not only blow away 14 years of discipline and pride and training, it would also give Lieutenant Roger Durnaway something to think about.

He pulled the pin, keeping the spoon depressed, and turned.

Lieutenant Roger Durnaway was in the tent-opening, silhouetted against the light from inside. He was shouting; in fact, screaming with rage. It was the first time Olsen had seen him express any really strong emotion. And the last, he thought, as he tossed the grenade. He dived sideways into a depression in the ground.

The grenade must have hit Durnaway in the stomach and dropped to the ground directly in front of him, because after the bang and the sudden angry glare and the clattering of debris on the ground, there wasn't a hell of a lot left of him.

The ironical part about the whole affair was that the guy who blew the whistle—the guy who happened to see the entire action and sang like a bird to the CID when they came nosing around, on being informed that there'd been no VC activity that evening within five miles of the hootch area—was Isaacs.

Isaacs—who'd figured in his weird way that telling the tale would enable him to work out some kind of deal to get him back to the World and the fresh-dug grave of his great-aunt.

Which, in the event, was precisely what it didn't do.

77

Dempsey snapped the file closed, placed it on top of the rest, and said, 'Right!'

He picked up the pile and held it in both hands, as though weighing it. He smiled.

'Plenty of jism here, Alkine. Yes, *sir*! A whole crotting load of it! This one, Alkine, goes straight through. We have an all-systems-go situation right damn here.'

He put the bundle back down on the desk-top and stood up, stretching himself. He lit another cheroot and puffed at it contentedly.

'You recall the corporal we used on the Lhon Nu job?' he said. 'What was his damn name?'

Alkine recalled very well. The Lhon Nu job had been when the cars of three prominent South Vietnamese peace activists had exploded at exactly the same time in three different parts of the city. With the three prominent South Vietnamese peace activists inside them. The CIA-controlled *Saigon Post*, commenting on the outrage, had pointed out that this was exactly what you'd expect from VC terror-bombers: they didn't give a shit who they blew up. Or words to that effect.

'Yes, sir. Donaghy.'

'Prime him, Alkine. We're gonna be needing his expertise right soon.'

'Sure thing, General.'

'You see about a pilot . . . gunners?'

'No, sir. You said . . .'

'Forget it. Stocker'll have some ideas on that score.'

Alkine wriggled uneasily in his seat.

'About Stocker, General. D'you really think . . .'

He was interrupted by the buzz of the intercom.

'I have Sergeant Stocker here, General.'

'So send him in,' said Dempsey. He glanced at Alkine, who resolutely refused to meet his gaze.

Sergeant Alvin Stocker was in his early-30s, tall and big-boned. His chin was smooth and solid and spade-shaped. He had light blue eyes and a small, pursed mouth, out of all proportion to his chin. He looked as though he chewed limes whole, and plenty of them.

He saluted, stiffly erect, his chin out, his head well back, staring at nothing.

Dempsey clapped him on the shoulder, pushed him towards one of the chairs against the wall. Stocker sat on it, still staring out into the illimitable distance.

'Loosen up, Sergeant,' said Dempsey genially. 'God-damnit, we're all crapping friends here. We all squat on the same shitter. Isn't that right, Alkine?'

'It certainly is, General,' said Captain Alkine in a voice from which every mote of emotion had been extracted.

PART TWO

I

In the half-light of early evening the Huey looked like a big-eyed, fat-nosed bug from front on. It looked as though it ought to crawl along the ground with extreme difficulty, painfully, not hurtle and soar through the skies like a great bird of prey.

Hot and perspiring, Hardin dismissed this thought and wondered why in hell they were giving him a Huey in the first place. A gunship. A Goddamn killing machine. This was strictly a commercial flight. It made no sense.

But then nothing that had happened to him over the past three days made sense. First an out-of-the-blue order to get himself up to Da Nang fast, which he'd accomplished by hopping a C-130 transport from Bien Hoa at short notice, then, on arrival, he'd found he had to carry on up to Hue. There, he'd discovered there'd been some Admin foul-up, and he had to return to Da Nang, and now he was to head down south again to Special Forces HQ at Nha Trang, via, for Christ's sake, Pleiku.

For a moment Hardin thought that maybe it was Dempsey, somehow pulling strings to keep him occupied, keep him on the move. Maybe when he arrived at Nha Trang he'd find he had to jump on down to Bien Hoa again then back up to, Jesus, Loc Ninh, or Da Lat, or someplace like that. Maybe all this jumping up and down was some kind of piss-bucket revenge on Dempsey's part, just to show Hardin that Dempsey was a general and Hardin was a colonel and you didn't say no to a general however corrupt and venal he was and however much dirt you had on him.

Maybe. Then again, maybe not. Maybe it was simply a case of gears not meshing properly in the chain of command.

Whatever the hell it was Hardin wished someone'd stop using him like a yo-yo and send him back to the jungle. That was where it was good to be, and that was where he wanted to be. There, you were your own man; you relied on no one but yourself. There was no paperwork, no secondary duties, no chain of command; there was just you—watchful, wary, taking nothing for granted, living on adrenalin, surviving. There was no place on earth like the jungle, and there was no feeling in man's emotional experience akin to trying conclusions with death and passing the test with flying colours.

In fact there was no other way of passing that particular test; there were no half-measures. If you didn't pass it with flying colours, it meant you *were* dead.

Hardin shrugged, breathed out irritably. He'd been too long away from that green dreamworld where fantasy was reality, and beauty was death. He strode on towards the chopper.

'Colonel Hardin? I'm Lowadnik.'

Hardin acknowledged the man's salute. Lowadnik was beanpole-like with a carrot thatch. He had freckles, a good-natured expression on a thin face, and couldn't have been more than 20 at the outside.

'Don't mind me saying so, sir, but you're travelling light.'

Hardin grinned and patted the slim briefcase under his left arm.

'Where I'm going, Lieutenant, this is all I'll be needing.'

Lowadnik raised an eyebrow as he ushered Hardin into the chopper. Hardin nodded to the two door-gunners and went up into the nose, where the co-pilot was settling in.

'You mind if you travel cargo?'

'Uh ... nossir. That is, if Lew ... uh, Lieutenant Lowadnik...'

'He won't.'

'Nossir. Uh ... yessir.'

The co-pilot scrambled back to the main cabin and Hardin heard Lowadnik say, 'Man, he's a cool dude. You see the gear he's carrying? Like, zero!'

Hardin wondered idly what sort of gear you were supposed to take down to Pleiku. As he strapped himself in, he glanced at the controls. Lowadnik seemed like a pleasant guy; maybe he'd let him pilot this bird. It'd break the monotony. On the other hand, maybe he'd just catnap.

He needed some rack-time.

Lowadnik climbed into his seat and belted in. He gestured at Hardin's seat.

'S'okay by me, sir. But I take it you, uh . . . have driven one of these birds?'

'Well, I don't exactly carry a licence around with me, Lieutenant, but if you get your head shot off, providing I don't get my hands shot off, the rest of your crew should make it back home in one piece.'

Lowadnik grinned. Hardin had said the right thing in the right way. Lowadnik, like most pilots, was superstitious; thought it good luck to tempt fate before take-off. He'd read somewhere that German pilots, in some damn war or other, used to throw the greeting *'Hals und Beinbruch!'* at each other when they met. It meant, Break your neck and leg. Lowadnik liked that. It was cool.

He set the throttle and pushed the starter button with his thumb. A low whine gradually built up and rose, there were a couple of coughs, and the rotor overhead stirred into life, beginning to turn lazily like an old-fashioned ceiling fan. Then it quickened into invisibility, the turbine taking hold with an ear-splitting bellow. Lowadnik pulled up on the collective lever, and the Huey heaved up, tilted smoothly, then climbed into the air.

Lowadnik eased on the cyclic and touched the pedal, taking the chopper into a long circle to the left. Hardin looked out of his side-window. Darkness had come down fast; there were now lights to be seen below all over the air-base. He idly watched two brilliant beams turn round in a half-circle then disappear beneath him at speed: two trucks racing each other? He yawned, shifted his body into as comfortable a position as it could find. Lowadnik grinned at him.

'You settle right there, Colonel,' he yelled. 'Ain't gonna need a nav for this one. Done it too many times before.'

He made his forefinger and thumb into a circle and held it up, as though he was aping a member of East Coast high society drinking a cup of English tea.

'Could do it with my eyes shut, Colonel. And Charlie ain't gonna be expecting us this early. We're gonna be skating all the way!'

'Not many VC round Pleiku, Leiutenant!'

Lowadnik's face twisted up into a puzzled wince. He leaned towards Hardin, half-lifting one side of his helmet the better to hear.

'What was that, sir?'

'Forget it.' Hardin shook his head. He was too tired to carry on this screamed conversation. He placed his hands in his lap and let his knees sag outwards. He drifted off.

*　　*　　*

He emerged from sleep smoothly, all his senses alert, but with the nagging feeling deep-down that the gears were still not meshing correctly; that something was wrong somewhere, askew.

He opened his eyes and saw only darkness ahead, thick and black and impenetrable. Nor were there any lights to be seen when he peered through his side-window, narrowing his eyes in an effort to pierce the ebon void. He glanced at his watch. ETA was in about five minutes, and total darkness was not what he should be seeing. At all. He turned to Lowadnik.

'Where's Pleiku?' he shouted.

Lights on the instrument panel showed Lowadnik's puzzled expression.

'Back where it's always been, I guess, sir. Right back in Nam.'

For a second this failed to register with Hardin, then he lunged sideways, grabbing at Lowadnik's arm and at the same time jerking his own .45 automatic from its hip holster and releasing the safety.

'*Where the hell are we?*'

The chopper nose-dived some way before Lowadnik was able to correct it. He glared at Hardin.

'What the hell is this, Colonel?'

'Damn it, Lowadnik, you tell me where we're heading or I'll blow your Goddamn head off!'

Puzzlement turned to panic on the pilot's face.

'For Christ's sake, sir, we're heading where we've always been heading—drop-zone in Southern Laos!'

Shit, thought Hardin, I've been fingered. I've been Goddamned fingered and this poor fucker doesn't know what the hell is going on.

'Turn back!' he yelled. 'Turn back right now and head for the border fast!'

And then he thought: No, that's not the way it's going to be. Dempsey would've thought of that. He would've figured out the sequence of events damn near exactly the way it would go and keyed in a finale from which there'd be no escape.

Which is demonstrated, he thought, as the bark of an explosion hit his ears and the chopper lurched forward on its nose, bucking like a crazy horse. His seat-straps bit into him, jabbing the breath out of his body, and involuntarily he squeezed the trigger of his gun, sending a couple of bullets into the plexiglass window and adding to the hammering din of the rotors.

He heard Lowadnik scream *'Christ! We're hit!'*—and then the noise rose to pandemonium level as the chopper ploughed into the tops of trees, its rotors shearing into wood and topgrowth, and half-somersaulted before plunging downwards with a tremendous racketing roar.

Something smashed into Hardin's forehead and he blacked out for several seconds. When he came to he was upside down, but still strapped in, and all around him was blackness and silence and the strong and evil smell of aviation fuel. He was still clutching his automatic.

His fingers scrabbled round, caught at a projection of some kind. He holstered his gun and thumbed his harness button. Released, he slid sideways, clinging on to any firm piece of metal he could find.

He put a hand out for where Lowadnik ought to be, but all his fingers came into contact with were bits of broken branches and foliage. There didn't seem to be a front window any more. He turned and scrambled towards the rear, and found himself in the main cabin, on the ceiling. There was no rocking or shaking as he moved; what was left of the Huey seemed to be firmly wedged, probably as far down as the midgrowth of the forest.

Someone was groaning to his left, and his outstretched hand touched fatigue material.

'This is Hardin,' he said. 'Who's that?'

85

'Kelso . . . the co-pilot, sir.'

'You damaged?'

'Nossir. My head hurts is all.'

Hardin's night vision was beginning to shift into gear; he could make out thicker patches of black against various shades of a lighter greyness. The stink of fuel was very strong.

'The gunners?'

'Dunno about Finn, sir, but Lederer got the full blast.' His voice quavered. 'Jesus, sir, the full fucking blast. He was right up back. Jesus, he didn't stand a . . .'

'You got a gun?'

'Nossir. It's up front.'

'The hell with that. We have to get out of here.'

Hardin's instinctive response to this disaster was to move fast, as far away from the wreck as possible and in the shortest possible time.

'We got a radio back here?'

'God, I dunno, sir. It's all up front.'

'Shit.' Hardin crawled towards what ought to have been the port doorway and found a thick branch blocking his way. 'C'mon. Let's move.'

'You think there might be tigers out there, sir?'

'Worse than tigers, Kelso. Now haul ass. We might have a long climb.'

In fact, the Huey had stopped its headlong dive about 15 feet from the ground, and Hardin was able to scramble down to the thick lower branches then slide down the rest of the way to the jungle floor. The first thing he found was the second gunner lying in a twisted heap at the foot of the tree. He'd been thrown out hard and had landed on his head; his neck was broken.

Kelso came clattering down, and Hardin started to review the situation.

First and foremost, he had no food, and very little equipment worth a damn. He had his automatic, some clips of ammunition, and a knife he always wore—double-edged with an eight-inch blade. This was useful, but by no means optimum. You needed more than a gun and a knife to get yourself out of the jungle; anyone who thought otherwise was thinking in comic book terms. Maybe

Sergeant Rock could do it, or Sergeant Fury and his Howling Commandos, but those fuckers existed in a world where you didn't need quinine, sugar, salt tabs.

'Medical pack?' he said to Kelso.

'Nossir. It's all upstairs.'

Hardin shook his head. They could have spent an hour searching for survival equipment up in the treacherous blackness of the chopper, and the fact was he didn't even want to be here for ten minutes. In any case, all it needed up there was one tiny spark—one piece of metal dislodged and grinding against another—and it was fireball time.

'D'you know where the hell we are?'

He was very close to Kelso, and in the dimness he could just make out the look of astonishment that flitted across the man's face.

'Don't *you*, sir?'

'Never mind that. Where were we supposed to be heading?'

'A landing-zone we've used before, sir. On missions like this. Maybe five miles south of the Kong river. Lew could . . .'

'Do it blindfold, yeah. It may interest you to know, Kelso, that I was under the strong impression we were headed for Nha Trang, via Pleiku.'

'But, sir . . .' Kelso was beginning to stutter in his agitation. 'I mean, that's crazy, sir. I mean we had definite. I mean. Christ, you are Colonel John Hardin, aren't you, sir?'

'That's exactly who I am,' said Hardin, not even trying to suppress the rising fury in his voice, 'and this shithole is exactly where I'm supposed to be. Only trouble is, Kelso, I had no prior knowledge of it.'

'I just don't understand you, sir.'

'To put it bluntly, Kelso, I've been set up. And it's just tough shit on you that we're in the same Goddamn boat. You ever been in the jungle?'

'Nossir. Not . . . kind of . . . like this, sir. Not in this situation.'

Hardin reached forward and took hold of Kelso's shoulder, his fingers digging in deep.

'Now you listen to me, Kelso, and listen hard. If we're

87

anywhere near where you figure we are, we have maybe 50 miles of hostile jungle to plough through before we get back to Nam. Hostile in every Goddamn sense of the word you can think of. And even when we cross the border we're not, har-har-har, out of the fucking wood yet. So you just grab hold of that fact and ram it into your brain. You do everything I do, and everything I say, and you do it right damn fast. And maybe—just maybe—we might make it back in one piece.'

Kelso swallowed noisily and nodded.

Hardin squatted down, his fingers sifting through moss and leaves and undergrowth until he found a medium sized stone. He padded over to the gunner's body and tore off a long strip of shirt material, tying most of it round the stone, but leaving a length dangling from it. He moved back to Kelso, and brought out his lighter, setting fire to the cloth, watching it intently until the material was burning fiercely. Then he took hold of the dangling strip, whirled the flaming object round his head and sent it hurtling upwards towards the black bulk of the crashed chopper.

There was a dull and sullen-sounding thump and the darkness was ripped apart by an explosion of white light. Even where they were, the two men gasped as a blast of heat washed down at them, searing the air in their lungs. Then the light died to an orange glare, and ammunition began popping. Half-charred wood and bits of metal came clattering down through the branches.

Hardin breathed out in a gusty sigh and wiped sweat from his face. He gestured at Kelso. In the brief glare of the explosion he'd noticed something the other side of the burning wreck, and hoped to hell he hadn't been mistaken.

He wasn't. Lying just inside the circle of flickering light cast by the fire was Lowadnik. Or what was left of him. He was not good to look at. Hardin figured he must have been hurled through the front screen while the rotors were still turning . . . still chewing their way down into the foliage at tree-top level. Lowadnik had been flung into the rotors, and they'd sheared his head off and most of his shoulders and the whole of one arm. The torso lay in a wide scarlet pool where his blood had simply gushed out. Blood still ran even now, though sluggishly.

Hardin knelt down, slid the body over on to its back and unlooped the belt. He heard Kelso gagging behind him, and thrust the belt together with its holster up at the man. Then he thrust his hand under Lowadnik's shirt and gave a grunt of satisfaction as he felt a strip of elasticated cloth tight to the skin.

It was what he'd been hoping for—praying for, maybe. Had Lowadnik been a careful man? He didn't look the type, but you never knew. And now Hardin did know. Lowadnik had been a wise and careful man. He'd picked up hints from the men he ferried back and forth across the border. He'd learned lessons.

Hardin unsnapped the fastening and slid the narrow body-wrap from out under the torso. By the light of the fire he checked its contents. There were pockets in the wrap, each containing medical necessities of one sort or another: elastic bandages, slim tubes of antiseptic cream, a syringe in sections, each section in sealed sterilised plastic buds, morphine, barley sugar cubes, quinine, vitamin tablets, Benzedrine, strips of wadding.

Hardin smiled, almost wolfishly. He lifted his shirt and fixed the wrap round his waist, taking care to see that those sections containing the more fragile items were at his sides, not front or back.

He searched Lowadnik's pockets, but apart from personal papers and an ammunition clip there was nothing more. He passed the clip to Kelso, rolled the papers up into a thick ball and tossed it up into the fire above.

'Okay, let's move.'

He checked his watch. From the time they'd jumped down from the tree until now six minutes had elapsed.

Thank Christ I'm wearing good boots, he thought, as he stepped out into the tangle of undergrowth ahead. The clothes they were wearing were not true jungle outfits— not made of the heavy canvas that provided warmth at night and breathed during the day—but they ought to see them through. Apart from unfriendly forces, it was possible that the worst thing they might have to put up with would be assault by insects, continuous and ferocious. Kelso was already slapping at his face and muttering curses. Hardin turned.

'You'll have to hack it, Kelso. You'll just have to let those little fuckers eat you.' He squatted down and pulled Kelso with him. They were amidst a shrubbery of densely packed ferns that rose to a height of eight feet or more. 'You say we're maybe five miles south of the Kong river?'

'Well, about that, sir. I mean we never reached the actual LZ, and I guess I wasn't taking too much notice of anything in the back. But judging by my watch, hell, we were damn near on-target.'

A memory had just tugged at Hardin's mind.

'You ever hear of a ville called Mek Lonh?'

'Sure, sir. It's a safe ville. East along the river. Most of the Special Forces we ferry strike north or west, but if things go down the tube they know they can hole up there, use it as a jumping-off place for the border.'

Hardin pondered this. The fact was, there was no such ville as a truly safe ville: a village headman would welcome you one day, feast you, accept your gifts, hide your survival caches, and see you off the next morning with a smiling face—and perform exactly the same duties for an NVA force the following afternoon. There was nothing hypocritical in this: village honchos were wise men. If they refused the Americans they might find themselves with a burned out shell of a village in short order; if they refused the EnVees the same would apply.

But there was another factor to be taken into consideration. Dempsey had mentioned Mek Lonh, and that could be super-bad.

Or ... it could simply mean it *was* a reasonably 'safe' ville and Dempsey had chosen it as a pickup post because it would be cool for the guy who'd be doing the picking up.

Hardin wished he'd worked this area before, wished he knew the lie of the land. But it was no good thinking that way. The point was, a semi-friendly ville was better than no ville at all, which might be the case if they simply struck east now.

'Okay,' he said, 'we'll head for it. We'll go north until we hit the river, then east. It'll take us out of our way, but in the long run we could be doing ourselves a favour.'

As they moved on through the steamy darkness, Hardin wished he really believed that.

II

General Dempsey was on the phone, and that, thought Alkine, watching him, meant he was almost in his natural element.

Dempsey disliked the personal touch in his various extra-curricular activities, the face-to-face confrontation (unless it was to bawl someone out, but that was different). He preferred to be at least one step removed—better, three or four steps removed. He liked to keep well clear of his own affairs; liked, as he put it, to let others, more often than not Alkine, do the beavering. There were times, it was true, when circumstances drove him to take a personal—or, more accurately, physical—interest in a situation, but these occasions were rare; for the most part he maintained a profile that was so low as to be invisible.

Thus when, as now, he was forced to initiate a situation himself he felt safer if he could retain at least a semblance of this phantom state, and for this reason the telephone was a particularly useful tool. Dempsey respected the telephone; knew to the *nth* degree the power of the disembodied voice, and how fully to utilise that power.

Alkine had to admire him, even though he'd seen performances such as the one now being enacted too many times before.

'It's quite frankly a hell of a situation, Chip,' Dempsey was saying, a hunched and bulky figure, the phone rammed into his right ear, leaning over the desk and frowning down at its surface as though in deep, almost cataplexic shock. 'Believe me, I know it.'

Alkine pushed gum into his mouth and stared dully at the window and the darkness outside. He felt tired and dispirited; washed out. Now he knew exactly what Dempsey had in mind he wished the operation was over, was just a bad memory of something that had happened months ago.

'Soon as I got the word,' said Dempsey, 'I put my best men on it. Sure, I could've bounced a whole Goddamn squadron across the border within moments, but you know right damn well, Chip, this is a sensitive one. Sensitive area, sensitive man. Hardin has one hell of a bunch of scary stuff in his head—he knows one hell of a lot of things the EnVees'd chop their balls off for.'

Not to mention, thought Alkine bleakly, a hell of a lot of things good old Chip and his top brass'd chop *Dempsey's* balls off for, if they ever got to know about them.

'No, no, no, Chip. With all due respect, I have to say I believe a prejudicial wipeout should only be considered as an extreme last resort. Hell, Chip, we want to save the guy, not kill him! Well sure—if he's still alive to be saved. But that's something we just don't know, Chip. His mission?'

Dempsey stopped talking for maybe two seconds. Then he started again, his expression unaltered by even the tic of a muscle.

'Solo strat, Chip. Because of, uh ... future redeployments, which you know about, our side of the border, I felt it might be useful to have someone up there to monitor the area. Hardin seemed the right man for the job. His track record's a fine one, Chip. Really fine. A capable and courageous man. One of my best. To be frank, Chip, on the mission like this I'd normally make it a three-man team, but Hardin's a loner. Prefers the solo recon. So I let him do it the way he wanted. Hell, Chip, you know the way I operate. I like to keep the men happy. Give 'em what they want, within reason, and you get solid results. Now then,' Dempsey coughed a couple of times, then cleared his throat, 'we have a rough fix on where his chopper seems to have gone down. I'm still chasing details, Chip, but from what I can gather they were on open channel and contact just cut out. Two options here, Chip, as I see it. They were either shot down or forced down. Either way, we have to know. Like I said, Hardin's a good man, and if he's survived he could make it back across the border either alone or with the chopper's crew, no problem. But we can't take that risk, Chip. He's too damn important. Like I said, he's got a lot of Goddamn details in his head, and it'd be a hell of a propaganda coup if the EnVees captured him. What's that, Chip?'

Alkine grudgingly thought: This is a classic exercise, Dempsey's just let the old turkey have a stick to beat him with. He's stressed Hardin's importance ... stressed the fact that he knows maybe too much about Special Forces to be allowed to roam around the jungle on his own any more. So the old turkey is going to rap Dempsey's knuckles for that, and Dempsey is going to let him, and the old turkey is going to be satisfied with that and'll dismiss the whole damn business from his mind as soon as he puts the damn phone down. Jesus.

'Well, you could very well be right, Chip. I know exactly what you're saying. And maybe it is time we ought to think about pulling Hardin back on to Admin or something like that. But Goddamnit, Chip, with all due respect, you do not, repeat not, just go out and pick guys like Colonel John Hardin up off a street corner. They are like Goddamn gold-dust, Chip, with all due respect. Still, that isn't the point at issue, but I'll certainly bear in mind what you say very strongly, Chip. Now, in the time I've had since the news came through, I've already given the matter a great deal of thought, and ...'

Dempsey suddenly sat back in his chair, a faintly contented expression on his face.

'Well, that's right damn square of you, Chip, to say that. Right Goddamn square. Okay, so my feeling is that I should send in a force to pull Hardin out. A very special force, Chip. Very muscular. Because we don't want any more foul-ups with this one, right? They'll find Hardin or, if the worst comes to the worst, his corpse. Because we have to take that factor into consideration, of course, lousy as it may be. Still, we'll jump that boulder when we get to it—right, Chip? Sure, sure. I'll be pushing the go-button on this just as soon as I put the phone down. Great, Chip. Fine. And you send my best regards right back to Marge, you hear?'

Dempsey put the phone down and stood up, breathing deeply. He tapped the desk-top with a spatulate finger.

'Get it moving, Alkine. I want that bunch assembled fast and the chopper warming up for the off.' He suddenly stared at his subordinate narrowly. 'You don't look convinced, Alkine. Not at all.'

'It's just that this operation's been mounted at such a hell of a speed, General. There seem to me to be so many imponderables.'

'Like what?'

'Well . . . the squad, sir. Sure, I know we have the clout to pull them out of the stockade, but, hell, sir, someone is surely going to smell something cooking somewhere.'

Dempsey laughed harshly.

'So what if they do? The paperwork alone'd sink any long-nosed fucker who tried to work out what was going on. You know how the minds of these Remington Raiders work: if a job takes more than ten crapping minutes, forget it.' He suddenly leaned over the desk, whipping off his glasses and waving them at Alkine. 'How long the fuck have you been working for me?'

Alkine's brain-relays clicked into action.

'Four years, three months, and a couple of days, General.'

Dempsey's features became immobile, mask-like.

'I figure you have some idea what I'm getting at, Alkine.'

'I take you to mean, General, that over those four and a quarter years I have performed some highly delicate missions and taken part in a large number of extremely sensitive operations.' He paused. 'On your behalf.'

'Extremely,' said Dempsey dryly. 'Don't let's piss around, Alkine. They could send you to the gas-chamber, some of the things you've pulled.'

Alkine's mouth had, quite suddenly, gone very dry.

'With all due respect, General—the things *we've* pulled.'

Dempsey's smile was as genial as fly-spray.

'Don't shit in your pants, Alkine. You're safe. What I can't figure out is why, after four and a quarter years, you suddenly get fidgetty.' He pushed himself back up to a standing position again, gestured dismissively with his right hand. 'So someone bitches about this business—who cares? Intelligence is a hard wall to bang your crapping head against, Alkine. This is a dirty force for a dirty mission. That's the way we play it. And when it does go wrong—well, ain't that just too Goddamn bad.'

'I just hope it doesn't go right, General.'

Dempsey smacked the files that were still lying on his desk.

'With this bunch of dead-heads? Sweet Jesus, Alkine, I'm

94

really beginning to think you're losing your crapping nerve. And that's something you can't afford to do.'

'With all respect, sir, we don't even know if Hardin's dead. He *could* be alive.'

Dempsey shrugged.

'Whatever we do or don't know, one thing's for sure. Donaghy blew that chopper. That's a fact. And even if Hardin survived, the area he's in is stiff with hostiles, and he'd have to be Mr Goddamn Miracle to get through unfucking-scathed. Why the hell d'you think I had him hopping up and down Vietnam—for the good of his crapping soul? He's been on the move for nearly three days, non-stop—no equipment, not much food, damn little sleep. If he's down, he's had it!'

He began to stride up and down the room behind his desk, his movements confident, assured.

'So, just to show willing, we send out a rescue party. Which just happens to consist of trash from the bottom of the can. Junkies, deadbeats, jarheads—real no-hopers. You think they're going to save the day, like in Goddamn *Wagon Train*? No way, Alkine—no *way*!'

Dempsey stopped behind his chair and gripped the back of it tight, with both hands. His voice was low.

'None of these shitheads is coming home, Alkine. I've staked too much on this, and that's the way it's gonna be. Not one man is going to drag himself out of the jungle at the end of the day to tell the tale.'

III

Hardin sucked at a barley sugar cube and wished he had something that had more body to it. Like a dried apricot, or a fig. Barley sugar was fine, gave you energy, but it didn't last too long. A piece of dried apricot kept you amused for hours.

He stared at the darkness and felt the rain hammer down through the branches of the tree he was leaning against on to his unprotected head.

It had started an hour and a half, maybe two hours, before. First a cessation of even those sporadic noises you heard in the jungle at night—the grunt of a tiger, the unexpected crash of something moving in a nearby thicket, odd rustlings and crackings—then a slow, unevenly paced smacking sound, like the snapping of wood that has not been dead for long, and the sudden shock of a large drop of water thudding down on to your shoulders or back. Then more drops, falling at a faster rate, the sounds they made as they hit leaves and foliage growing louder, until there was nothing to distinguish between sound and action, and it was as though someone was emptying a bottomless barrel of water straight down on top of you.

The first time he had experienced this furious onslaught, six years ago, it had appalled him. He couldn't believe it was happening; couldn't believe that Nature had such a weapon at its disposal. The force of the rain was so strong that Hardin had suddenly understood what it must be like to be a nail slammed repeatedly by a hammer. It literally pounded you. Sometimes, at the height of the season, this pounding went on for days, weeks, non-stop: a ceaseless and soul-destroying barrage.

A far cry from the rains that fell on the woods of Vermont, up around Lake Champlain, where he'd played as a child and grown up. Those, surely, were softer rains, somehow cleaner and sweeter-smelling—especially in the fall, the dying of the year, when they pattered on the mosses and ground foliage, releasing strange and heady fragrances into the cool, sharp air.

Here, across half a world, the smell that exploded into the air was more often than not of death: the stench of rot and decay.

And yet there was beauty here, too. After a night's rain, as the sun came up and the jungle became a glittering wonderland of sparkling reflections; an unbelievably sudden and dramatic blaze of exotic colours when you rounded a bend in the trail; the thousand different shades of the colour green, all of them lush; the extravagantly-hued birds that hurtled in front of you and vanished out of sight, their long whooping shrieks dying into the cavernous silence.

It didn't last though. Nothing did here. As the sun rose in the vast azure vault of the sky so did the steam as the jungle dried itself off. And with the steam came the soggy heat and mosquitoes and slithering kraits and the all-pervading stench of corruption.

It was a place of bizarre and terrifying contrasts, and that, he knew, was precisely what fuelled his longings to return, again and again.

The rain was easing off now, he noted. Soon it would be time for them to move. Dawn was not far away, and Hardin wanted to reach the river before midday, and the village of Mek Lonh before nightfall. Long before nightfall. He would, he knew, need at least an hour to patrol the perimeters, sniff out the ground, check and double-check the villagers' movements from a safe distance. Only a fool or a madman walked into a safe ville with open arms and a big smile on his face without taking such precautions.

His mind drifted to Kelso. It was difficult to guess how he would make out. He could feel that man's weight on his right shoulder as they leant back against the bole of the tree, and it occurred to him that maybe, subconsciously, Kelso was trying to extract some kind of courage, or at least reassurance, from this close contact. That did not bode well for the future.

Hardin shifted his position slightly, and the pressure on his shoulder suddenly eased as Kelso lurched away from him in the darkness, falling with a dull smack on to the soggy earth.

A fine start to a beautiful relationship, thought Hardin

wryly. The kid's gone to sleep on me. If he keeps doing that, I have problems.

He stooped, feeling for him, his arms wide as his finger trawled through rain-slick grass.

'Kelso! Wake up!'

His searching hands found and grasped the man's boots, and he shook them gently, but got no response. He fished out his lighter and, cupping it against the fine drizzle that was now seeping down, snapped it on, holding his arms out over where the man's head ought to be.

He saw, in the brief flare of light that was all he allowed himself, that Kelso was smiling.

But not with his mouth.

His mouth lolled open, the corners turned down. The smile was in the throat, a wide curving gash of vivid crimson from which blood still flowed in a thick stream across the man's chest.

Hardin didn't hesitate. A split-second was all he needed to take in the sight before he dropped the lighter and instinctively whirled round in a half circle at the crouch and drove himself forward with all the strength and speed and ferocity he could muster—feeling a tingle of almost malicious satisfaction ripple through him as his head sank into heavy cloth and yielding flesh. The man who had waited for him to crouch down by the body and had padded up behind him so horrifyingly silently went down with hardly a grunt. Hardin was already tugging at his knife, and now, grabbing a flailing arm with one hand to steady his target, he drove the eight-inch blade savagely into the man's abdomen, twisted it, then heaved it up at an angle, shearing through soft tissue until it crunched against the rib-cage. Blood spouted hotly over his face, spurting into his eyes and momentarily blinding him.

It made no difference. Hardin's innate killer-skill and instinct for survival told him what to do . . . told him to within a centimetre where he should strike. The knife came out, fast and smooth, and stabbed down again, plunging deep into the man's heart.

Again the knife came slickly out, and Hardin dived sideways, rolling desperately through grass and stunted bushes heavy with water, until his shoulder slammed into the thick roots of a tree. He caught at the roots and jerked himself at the trunk, curling round it in a swift slither until he was on its furthest side. He sprang to his feet, now making no sound at all. He flattened himself against the tree. He waited.

Incredibly, in that brief space of time since Kelso had crashed to the ground beside him, the rain had ceased and the darkness had begun to lift perceptibly. To his right he could just see a paper-thin band of light in the far distance, broken at irregular intervals by the black shapes of trees. That meant only one thing. He was on high ground, very near to where it fell away down to a valley. Probably a river valley. The Kong river valley.

His mouth was not dry, and his heart was beating at only a fraction over its normal rate. For the first time in many days he felt alert, at full stretch, alive—and it was ironical that he should feel this way after he'd just killed a man. Perhaps death—the taking of life, violently—*was* what truly motivated him? Perhaps it *was* his sole incentive as a human being? Hardin shoved this thought out of his mind. Time enough to sort that out, if he remembered (as he never did), after he'd made his second kill.

Because there had to be a second kill. He knew without the minutest shadow of a doubt that there was at least one other man standing quite still—or crouching, or lying down, or fixed in some other frozen attitude—not ten yards away from where he was.

He could hear nothing but the silence—and he knew that that would not last for very long. Soon that strip of light on the far horizon would expand to fill the whole sky, and long before that the jungle would be stirring, awakening into noisy life.

He turned his head slightly, his eyes flicking to left and right, trying to pierce the gloom. To the left he could just make out a thick tangle of undergrowth, then more trees; to his right bushes and the trunks of trees were more easily discernible, standing out in sharp contrast to the growing band of light. Nothing stirred.

He was making up his mind to initiate some kind of action when there was a rustling crash to his right. Instantly he recognised the sound for what it was—not someone moving in the bushes, but someone throwing a stone so that it *sounded* like someone moving in the bushes. Except that it never did.

Hardin smiled, almost sadly. That told him all he wanted to know. It told him there was only one out there, and whether it was male or female, it was very young and very inexperienced—because only a beginner would have tried the oldest trick in the book.

He'd bumped into the classic EnVee double-act. The regular taking the learner out on night-patrol—showing him how to move quietly, how to crawl so that nothing around you moved, how to set traps in the dark, how to keep silent and still for minutes at a stretch and not give your position away. How to be a guerilla.

It must have been, thought Hardin, a hell of a jolt for the regular to come across two Americans deep, as they were, into the Laotian jungle. And the perfect opportunity to teach the recruit the most important lesson of all—how to kill a man without making the slightest sound.

So he'd sneaked up on Kelso, who probably had been dozing, and slit his throat. Hardin had to admit the guy had been good—even allowing for the fact that the sound of the rain helped to mask the sound of his movements. But the guy had not been that good, or he would not now be lying where he was, with half his guts emptied out on to the sodden ground.

Hardin watched the bushes to his right intently, focusing his gaze on a spot just above them. He knew the kid had a fix on him, knew him to be behind this tree. He also knew that the kid was waiting for him to jump *right*—towards the bushes—if he made any move at all. And then the kid would nail him with a burst. Probably, because he was a learner, a hell of a long burst. Now Hardin wanted an exact fix on him.

This time he saw it—saw something curving through the air against the rapidly brightening skyline and vanish with a rustle into the undergrowth. From the angle of drop he knew almost precisely where the thrower had positioned himself. He jumped out left, round and away from the tree, holding the knife extended outward from him, like a sword, and uttering a harsh, blood-curdling shriek.

100

And saw there were two of them.

For a micro-second time stopped; the scene was frozen.

Hardin's wild leap had landed him two feet, no more, from a boy holding a Kalashnikov AK–47 assault rifle aimed at the tree—at the spot where Hardin ought to have emerged. Beyond him, across the small clearing, was a second boy, the thrower, in exactly the position Hardin had calculated. Both had whipped round at his appearance, and were staring at him, their faces masks of unbelieving horror. Even in the half-darkness Hardin could see that neither boy could possibly be more than 15 years old, if that.

But Hardin's lust for survival was instinctive, atavistic. It was him or them, and he lunged forward at the nearest boy, sweeping the knife round in a vicious but controlled half-arc. The blade sliced into the boy's throat, nearly taking his head from his shoulders as blood spouted into the air, drenching Hardin's arm and face. The second boy was already turning, starting to run, yelling with terror, but Hardin's knife-hand flew up and back, then hard down, and as if by magic the knife appeared in the boy's back, pitching him over with its punching impact.

Hardin stooped, grabbed the AK–47, and swung it up then round, his left arm as rigid as a steel tie, his eyes darting from left to right and back again, his breath now coming in short sharp gasps.

Nothing moved. Not a leaf stirred.

Hardin took air in through his nose like a drowning man, but he still did not relax. The boy at his feet was dead, but the other one . . .

Cautiously, he moved across the glade, went into the undergrowth at an angle.

Quite dead. The blade had buried itself in his back up to the hilt and had lanced straight through the heart. If the boy had been skinnier the knife's point would have come out the other side.

Hardin tugged the knife out and cleaned it, slipping it back into its sheath. It was now much lighter; he could see quite clearly without straining his eyes. Carrying the AK–47 he walked back to the tree under which he and Kelso had sheltered.

The dead regular was wearing an assault rifle as well, and Hardin compared the two guns, breaking both of them down into their three basic parts then reassembling them. He chose the regular's. Its distinctive banana magazine was scratched and scarred, and the stock was dented in a dozen places; it was a well-used piece of equipment. But it was very well maintained.

It was true that the US army's M–16 was lighter, fired faster, and had a greater effective range and hitting power over the AK–47, but given the choice Hardin would have taken the Kalashnikov every time. You could stomp on this baby, whack it against a tree, toss it under a truck, then pick it up and nail a low-flying gunship. Who cared that its accuracy was suspect above 300 yards? This gun could take a lot of shit, and still come up shooting.

He used the boy's AK to dig rough, shallow graves in deep undergrowth then hauled the bodies in, covering them with leaves and mud. He worked quickly, yet methodically, cleaning up as much of the blood that had been splashed around as he could see. He knew his survival depended on actions such as these.

When he'd finished he began to prowl around the bushes beyond the glade. There was something missing, and he had to find it; knew he could not move a step from the immediate area until he did find it.

He found it at last by tripping over it in the gloom—the regular's backpack. He checked through it quickly, sifting its contents, and in less than a minute he knew he was safe. There was not much inside, which meant that the regular and his two learners were on patrol of a night and a day. With a bit of luck another night after that. It was possible to calculate that they had come a distance of at least five miles from their starting-point, maybe more. No one, therefore, would start worrying about them for a couple of days.

It was possible, of course, that this had been their second night, but Hardin thought it unlikely, judging by the condition of a cluster of rice-balls he found inside the pack. He ate some of these, and kept the others for later. He thought about using the backpack, then rejected the idea.

Like the AK–47's combat superiority over the M–16, the NVA backpacks were much lighter, easier to haul, than their American counterparts, but Hardin knew he could carry all he wanted to carry on his own person, and the pack could prove a liability in a dangerous situation. He thrust it out of sight under a large bush.

He went over the equipment he now had: the AK–47, with a magazine belt across his chest; two .45 automatics (he'd taken back the one he'd originally given Kelso, adjusted the belt and strapped it round his own waist); spare clips for both handguns; his knife in its sheath. He also had the medical supplies and the rice-balls.

Now he relaxed and indulged in a brief fit of fury with himself, a few moments of self-disgust. This miscalculation back then could've cost him his life. It those two boys had been hardened, experienced NVA regulars, he'd be a dead man now.

And then he thought: but they *were* boys, and that was the luck of the game. I feel sorry for them, especially the one who knew real fear and ran, but it only needed one of them to kill me. And I survived.

Without a backward glance at the glade, he padded through the trees until he reached a point where the ground fell away in a gentle slope below him. Beyond lay a wide, jungle-choked valley, with a river running through it, twisting and turning, at times disappearing from sight, until it finally ran into and between wooded hills in the mid-distance.

At the horizon, far away, the sun was a great white ball of blinding light. The air was fresh and clean. He was on his own. Dempsey would not destroy him; he would destroy Dempsey.

He began to move down the slope.

IV

Leroy Vogt could not figure out what in God's name was going on.

They had come for him during the night, two burly, hard-faced MPs, thrown a suit of fatigues into his cell and told him to dress. The fatigues were made of heavy canvas, the kind that were used in the jungle. That hadn't made sense for a start.

Then they'd loaded him up with equipment. Jungle boots, water bottle, steel helmet, backpack, rations, even cigarettes. And M–16 clips. *M–16 clips*?

But no M–16. That was even stranger.

Then they'd given him a good—a very good—meal: soup, a massive T-bone steak with all the trimmings, apple pie and cream, all the coffee he wanted.

That was very very weird. So weird, in fact, that Vogt had to keep surreptitiously pinching himself to see if he really was awake. But it seemed he was.

Trouble was, he hadn't enjoyed the meal for worrying.

The court was a bad memory now; he wanted to forget it. But all this brought it back. First off, they'd hit him with a 'premeditated murder' charge. Witnesses came forward and said Vogt didn't like the way Sergeant Morelli treated him; that he was sullen and vindictive. Prosecution said that he'd planned the whole thing because Morelli used to bawl him out a lot.

Vogt had had some very bad moments then. But his defence lawyer, a young and businesslike captain who'd told Vogt that this was the sixteenth charge of 'premed' he'd had to deal with—in five months—was a sharp talker. And there was the girl, too. She was a solid act. Even Corporal Calhoun had had to admit that, yeah, maybe it might've seemed that the girl was some kind of refugee, and, yeah, it could've looked to an inexperienced guy like Vogt that Morelli was just going to, well, blow her away for no good reason.

So now all Vogt had to look forward to was years and years and years in the brig—because, sharp talker as the captain had been, he hadn't been able to get him off the hook completely.

'The courts,' he'd said, 'gung-ho. They're out for blood, son. Too much fragging going on out there these days, of one kind or another.' He'd glanced at his watch. 'Fact is, I've got another one in a half hour: real frag this time. Sergeant blew his lieutenant away. Shouldn't be too bad; the prick was a real martinet, and I can bring up mucho evidence to prove it. But that's not really the point. The Command don't see it that way. They want blood.' He'd shrugged. 'Sorry, Leroy.'

So—at least no death sentence. But now Vogt wasn't so sure. Maybe they'd reneged. You never knew with the military. Maybe all this good food was the meal the condemned man traditionally ate before they took him out.

But why the equipment? And, especially, why the M–16 clips?

No one answered any of his questions and when the meal was over he'd been bundled into a truck which contained three guards and one other guy, a skinny black, dressed like him and with the same equipment. The black looked worried, and no wonder. Vogt wondered if he looked the same, and thought he probably did. They were not allowed to speak—only look at each other and raise eyebrows and smile nervously.

The truck had dumped them a half hour later, while it was still dark, and their equipment was taken from them. Then they'd been pushed into a briefing-room where there were five other guys, all dressed the same. No one had any flashes on their fatigues at all.

There were a couple of solidly built guys, one with a friendly, crumpled face, now squeezed up into a puzzled expression, and blond, curly hair, while the other looked like he was some kind of boxer, maybe. He didn't look at all friendly, and kept glaring round the room, as if he might suddenly break out and smash the windows or throw the chairs around. He had the build for it, Vogt decided.

There was a tall, gangling guy who was, or seemed to be, totally relaxed; had his feet on one of the tables and was smoking. He didn't seem at all worried at being where he was, and maybe he had no reason to be. He was the only one who had on any sort of identification, if you could call it that—a medic's armband.

Of the other two, one was short and stocky with black hair. He kept on glancing around him, quickly and nervously like a bird, looking at the other guys, his eyes darting all over the room. He couldn't keep still, either; kept shifting about in his seat as his eyes flicked round. The seventh guy had light hair and a face that had no expression on it whatsoever. He sat quietly, staring in front of him at nothing; taking absolutely no interest in what was happening or in any of the other occupants of the room.

To complete the muster, four armed MPs stood guard: two by the door, one up on the lecture dais, the last one at the rear. But they didn't stay where they were for very long.

The door opened and a captain with Special Forces flashes carrying a clipboard came in, followed by a tall, blank-faced sergeant. The captain reached the dais, mounted it, and gazed at the seven men. It was clear to Vogt that he did not like what he was looking at. The sergeant jerked his head at the MP on the dais, who nodded and went out, his men after him. The door closed.

'My name's Captain Alkine,' said the captain. He gestured at the sergeant. 'This is Sergeant Stocker. You'll acknowledge your presence when I read out your names.' He glanced at the clipboard. 'Olsen.'

Near the front the big blond got to his feet, snapping smartly to attention. As he did this, the other heavyweight stood up too, but not to attention.

'Look, what the hell is this?'

The sergeant stepped down from the dais.

'Siddown,' His voice was low, flat-toned.

'Go fuck yourself . . .'

He got no further. Stocker's hand was already rising. Now it swung round in a vicious chop to the heavyweight's throat. He gagged, his face crimsoning as he lurched sideways, falling into a chair then crashing over it to the floor.

'We really don't have much time,' said Alkine, as though nothing had happened. 'Just answer your names and then listen to what I have to say. It's very simple.'

He continued round the men, ticking off their names on the clipboard as they answered. Vogt felt an odd sensation in his stomach as he listened, noting his companions' names. He knew two of them, or, at least, had heard of them on the brig grapevine.

O'Mara, now. Couldn't be two blacks with a name like that. This had to be the guy who strangled a colonel or a major with his own chains. Some kind of pervert. Or maybe it was the colonel or major that was the pervert. And Meeker, too. There was a lieutenant of that name who'd hijacked a gunship. Drew a gun on the pilot to get himself to safety, and left his men to die on a hot LZ. Then just gave himself up back at Base without a murmur. Really cool. Or stark crazy.

Oh my God, thought Vogt, what *is* this?

'You men are really very lucky,' said Alkine. 'You've all been given a second chance: a chance to get yourselves off the hook. You're being sent into the jungle to rescue a VIP. Sergeant Stocker here is in charge. All you have to do is follow orders, find your man, bring him back and,' he shrugged, 'that's it. No questions? Good.'

This last was said at speed; it was clear it was a formula Alkine felt he had to recite, merely for the record. Nevertheless, Pepper, the tall medic, got to his feet.

'Well, actually, there are a couple of . . .'

'Siddown,' said Stocker again. 'You don't have any questions. None of you punks have anything to say to anyone. From now on, you do what I say and you do it when I say it, and you don't piss around thinking about it.'

He rapped on the lecture-desk with his knuckles. The door opened and the MPs filed back.

'Get this trash out to the chopper,' said Stocker.

*   *   *

Out on the field dawn was coming up fast, attacking the darkness with a brilliant, sharp-edged brightness, chasing the stars into oblivion.

Stocker was beginning to feel excited. He was watching the squad lining up to climb into the chopper, but in his mind's eye he was seeing them lining up to be slaughtered.

Like beef in a stockyard.

He didn't want to do this one in cold blood. He didn't want it to be sudden, or unexpected. He wanted to see them gape with shock as he turned his M–16 on them; wanted to savour the terror on their faces. He could feel surges of excitement in the pit of his stomach, a sensation like a fist clenching and unclenching right down there in his groin. None of this showed at all on his face.

The MPs had gone. The only men here now were his: two door-gunners, a pilot and a co-pilot. Hand-picked men. Very carefully hand-picked, because they'd had to be shown the scenario, had to be told what was going to happen at the end of the ride.

Stocker gazed down at the tarmac, the corners of his pursed mouth twitching. It was really very amusing. They'd agreed to the job, and that meant they'd agreed to their own deaths. Stocker was going to get an enormous kick out of turning the M–16 on them when he'd finished off the squad. There were going to be bodies all over the jungle floor, all jumbled up together, and there was going to be a lot of blood.

Whenever Stocker thought the word 'blood', invariably the ditch at Tun Phouc sprang into his mind, in full sharp technicolour. Jesus, there'd been blood there, right enough.

The pity of it was that these punks weren't going to be wearing white. The damn green canvas they had on didn't show up the red so good. Stocker thought that maybe he could cripple them before taking them out completely. Shoot their damn legs away, or something, so they were immobilised, then strip their fatigues off somehow. *Then* rip 'em.

That might prove difficult, though; they might fight back. He'd have to think this one out very carefully.

He was suddenly aware that he was trembling.

'S'matter, Stock? Got the fever?'

It was the co-pilot, Endean. Stocker sniffed hard; controlled himself.

'Nothing. Nothing the matter with me.' He looked round; frowned. 'I thought Clode was here. Where in hell is Clode? This chopper's gotta be in the air.'

Endean shrugged.

'Haven't seen him this morning. He was taking tabs last night, but he said he'd be here. I guess he'll be here if he said he'll be here.'

'*Goddamnit!*' Stocker spat the word out as though it was a fly that had flown into his mouth.

'Uh-uh.' One of the gunners pointed at a figure loping towards them with long strides. 'Looks like we got us another pilot. Jesus, a black.'

'Fuck it, a captain, too,' said Endean. 'What do we do, Stock? You think Clode let him in on this?'

'Take him out,' muttered Stocker. 'When we get there, take him out.'

The black acknowledged their salutes. He was tall and thin, but muscular. He held a small hold-all in one hand and sun-glasses in the other. He grinned, turning to Endean.

'You Endean? Clode got sick; something really wild hit him in the night, what I heard. So you got me. Next on the rota. You better nav me right, baby, 'cos I sure as hell do not know where the fuck we is heading, except some dude fell down in the Big Green and we gotta haul his ass out.'

He stepped up into the chopper and climbed into the pilot's area, without even glancing at the men inside. There was no need to; all grunts look the same, and this was just another load of grunts to be ferried out to just another shitty situation. Nothing new under the sun. He yawned and then placed the bag on the left hand side of the seat, unzipping it quickly.

He folded his glasses over the cyclic and yawned again, this time stretching his arms right back hard above his head. He turned and peered back into the main cabin.

'Hey, Endean. You got the . . .'

He didn't finish what he was saying because he'd just spotted one of the grunts. Spotted, and recognised. His mouth dropped open. Then he lunged forward, grabbing the man by the throat.

Vogt was staring gloomily at the radio he'd just been handed when this happened. They still hadn't been supplied with M–16s yet; probably, he thought, because it was felt they weren't to be trusted with them until they

109

were down in the jungle. Though what difference being down in the jungle made he wasn't at all sure. Guy like the heavyweight Garrett could turn his gun on Stocker there as easily as anywhere else.

Now he looked up at the sudden disturbance and saw that the man the black captain was shaking so violently, almost as though he wanted to jolt his head right off, was the guy who'd been such a stone-face since the briefing-room. Only, right now, he was registering emotion like there was no tomorrow.

Only it wasn't, as one might have thought, discomfort or pain, so much as shock. No, more than that—outright terror.

'*Meeker*!' yelled Captain Frank Marco. 'What the fuck *you* doin' here, you pusillanimous little shit?'

Outside on the tarmac Stocker heard the commotion and reacted instantly. He glanced around, saw there was no one within two hundred yards of them, grabbed for his Armalite and jumped into the chopper.

'Back off, Captain.'

Marco didn't seem to notice.

'This mother the mother who held me up! Like fuckin' Jesse James! So what in God's name he doin' in this chopper? He was sent down, for Christ's sake. He was all set up to be locked away until the Second Coming, is what he was all set up to be locked away until. No way was this outrageous sonuvabitch of a trashbrained bandit gonna be let out. Not until the fuckin' millenium. *So why is he here*?'

Stocker jabbed the muzzle of the M–16 into Marco's ribs. 'I said, back off.'

Marco turned and looked at Stocker as though Stocker had just pulled the trigger and half of Marco's stomach was sailing away into the distance.

'Put that Goddamn gun down, Sergeant,' he grated. 'Your ass gonna get more than busted for this.'

Stocker shook his head, bleak-eyed. He half turned, still keeping his eyes on Marco's face and the rifle rammed into Marco's side.

'Dondell, McGerr—cover these fuckers. Any of 'em moves, waste 'em.'

The two gunners crowded the seven men to the rear of

110

the cabin with their rifles while Endean produced an automatic pistol. He pointed it at Marco.

'Better let him go, Captain. Stocker ain't fooling around. Just get up to your seat and let's go, okay?'

Marco slowly relaxed his hold on Meeker's throat, not even looking at the man as he scuttled away across the cabin to join the rest of the squad under Dondell's watchful eye and menacing Armalite. Instead Marco lifted a hand and let a long forefinger drag down his cheek, along the groove of a livid scar, still only partially healed.

'That's what that SOB did to me, with a pistol barrel. Nearly opened it to the bone. Hell, and I didn't even get to whup his hide when we got back to Base.' His eyes flicked from Stocker to Endean then back to Stocker again. 'You jus' tell me what the hell goin' on here, Sergeant. Once is squalid enough. Some bad shit was poured over me for that. Man gets to thinkin' God ain't on his side if he gets dumped on twice. In three months. Know what I mean?'

'Up front,' said Stocker. 'Endean'll nav for you. Don't rock the boat, Captain. You just might come out of this alive.'

Marco looked across at the grunts, took in their white, strained, uncomprehending faces. Then he took in the hardware that was ranged in on him. Then he took in Stocker's expression. Then he turned slowly towards the pilot's area.

'Fuckin'-A,' he said disgustedly.

V

Hardin had found the perfect hide—under a banana tree.

It was perfect for two very good reasons: its broad, cool leaves sheltered him from the full debilitating power of the sun, now climbing towards its zenith, and his position under it enabled him to look down into the centre of the hamlet of Mek Lonh without anyone spotting him. He was on a shrub-covered knoll topped by a banana tree plantation, and due to the nature of the shrub-growth below him he had a clear line of vision if he sat up straight, propped up against the curving trunk of the tree.

So far he had been here for half an hour. He had first circled the ville four times, very slowly, peering out at the backs of the huts and between them from various vantage points, and had decided that things looked cool. All he had to do now was wait, for maybe another half hour, and watch.

He'd been very impressed, first off, by the children. He was still impressed by them. There were lots of them, running, hopping, chattering, sitting around in the dirt and piling stones up into vague pyramid shapes then knocking them down again with shrieks of laughter. The more he watched the children, the more he became convinced this was a safe ville.

Maybe. You could never be entirely sure. But it was a good sign, all the same, seeing the children playing about freely and without any constraint.

Watch for the ville with children, he thought. Watch even more for the ville where the children are sitting too near the huts and staring into space, looking as though they'd like to play but daren't. Like a picture, or a posed photograph. Everything too prettified. Too neat. Too quiet.

That was the kind of ville you walked into in a column and got instantly cut down by interlocking fields of fire from maybe three machine gun posts in three separate huts firing over the kids' heads.

Mek Lonh did not seem to be that kind of ville. It was built in a long rectangle, one side open to the fields. To the rear was a wooded hill. It was typical of a thousand he'd seen: bamboo long-houses with thatch roofs, smoke from fires, mama-sans going about their mama-san business, papa-sans smoking and idly chewing the fat in one corner of the main plaza. You wouldn't think there was a war on.

Beyond a grove of trees to his left rice paddies stretched down towards the river, swollen now after the night's heavy rain. He could see, if he raised his head slightly, water-buffaloes moving slowly in a small herd and figures darting around them using sticks to goad them to move faster. Every so often one of the lumbering beasts bellowed irritably.

Hardin recalled a search-and-destroy operation in which he'd taken a part when the little yellow men had stampeded a herd straight at a platoon. The VC had run out of rounds and needed a diversion to cover their retreat. Some Goddamn diversion. Eight men trampled to death in the rush. And the rest were trying to blow the cows away with their M-16s and not having a hell of a lot of success, and the beasts were screaming mad with terror and pain, spouting blood all over the grass and raising dust so it was like looking at an advancing wall of solid fog. Those damn cows took a lot of killing. Hardin had felt more sick after that than at just about any other time he'd been in Nam. Hell of a mess.

But those darting figures down there were villagers. Unquestionably.

He'd already tagged the headman's hut: the one resting on stone piles with a verandah. An old mama-san was sitting on the lower steps, her head raised to the sky, taking in the sun.

Hardin made up his mind. His belly was growling, and the thought of the rice-balls didn't exactly excite the taste-buds. The ville was clean.

He glanced at his watch. Still, better to be safe than sorry. He'd give it another fifteen minutes.

113

VI

'There's something! Wreckage! Could be what we're looking for, Stock!'

Endean, still keeping the M-16 he'd swapped for his automatic trained on Marco, half-turned his head and yelled back at the main cabin.

Far below a darker mass of tangled and blackened machinery stood out against the lighter natural green of the trees. Around it were signs of a searing explosion: burnt foliage and charred branches. What was left of the chopper was nose deep in the trees, quite a way down.

Stocker came through.

'Take her round a little.'

Marco swung over the cyclic, touching the pedal to begin a turn to the left. He eased the collective down a little, and the gunship turned in a wide easy spiral, sinking down through the clear air towards the forest below. The altimeter sank back inexorably, then hovered as Marco stopped his descent. Under them, leaves and top-foliage shivered in the down-draught.

Endean put the muzzle of the M-16 to Marco's head, then both he and Stocker peered down.

'A blow-out,' said Endean. 'Must've exploded when it hit the trees. Tanks went up. Ain't no one survived that, Stock.'

'Don't look like it.' Stocker's eyes ranged beyond the immediate jungle, then he pointed. 'That looks likely— way over. Could be where there's a thin-out in the trees.'

'So?'

'So we head for it. If there's a clearing, we put down.'

Endean frowned.

'Why don't we heave these grunts out now, Stock? Climb to a thousand and just push the fuckers out.'

'No.'

'Hell, Stock, why not? Then we can fly back over the border and dump the chopper there. Jesus, we got a hell of a way to walk if we set down here.'

'*I said no!*'

Stocker still hadn't gotten over the lousy coincidence of this nigger pilot being the one Meeker had hijacked. The incident back at the Base had shoved everything out of gear. Stocker liked a smooth operation. Jobs that started fouled up had a nasty habit of ending up fouled up in his experience, and already this one was starting to shift uneasily out of sync.

'We got a long walk? Too bad. That's the way it's gotta be. There's a ville called Mek Lonh, east along that river down there. It's safe. There's a cache hidden there, left by Special Forces a month or so back. But whatever, we gotta come out of the jungle looking like shit.'

Endean shrugged.

'Sure, Stock.'

Marco nodded ahead.

'Good clearing. You wanna sit down?'

'Yeah.'

'An' what happens to li'l ole me then?'

'Just sit her down.'

Marco began spiralling again. The clearing was wide and ringed by tall trees; elephant grass grew over it in abundance. The altimeter began to sink again, and at 50 metres he began to feel the ground effect—as though he was sinking into slowly thickening molasses. The long grass swayed and bent and swirled around, flattened by the rushing wind of the rotors. Marco put the chopper down with only the slightest bump, locked the collective and set the cyclic at neutral. He sat back in his seat and stretched his legs out, turning his head very slightly but just enough to see that Stocker was already climbing back into the main cabin. Well and good. He surreptitiously checked his side-door.

Stocker jerked a thumb at the two gunners.

'Get 'em out.'

Dondell and McGerr pushed the seven grunts out of the port door, herding them away from the chopper. Marco had landed near the jungle, but most of them, who'd known what to expect as soon as the guns had been produced back at the Base, knew it was still too far to run to escape the withering hail of rounds that would be coming their way any second.

Garrett said, 'Look, what the fuck is all this in aid of? You don't have to kill me! I can be useful to you! *What is this*?'

Vogt felt very sick. His legs had become weak and his knees were trembling. He wondered what he'd done that the High Command had ordered him to be executed out here. Hell, as far as he could tell they weren't even in Vietnam!

Doc Pepper thought: I'm just gonna have to blank this off. Man, I could do with a hit right now.

Olsen said, 'You cannot do this, damn you. You cannot just do this!' He stepped forward, his fists raised, his face red with outrage. McGerr grinned and thrust the barrel of his gun into the big man's stomach, deep, shoving him backwards so that he staggered and fell.

O'Mara was desperately trying to pull his thoughts together in an attempt to pictorialise that after-hours session with Duane Allman. That had been so good, so crazy-good, so cool. He was trying to picture Allman as he crouched over his guitar. But it was a vain endeavour: he couldn't even remember what the guy looked like.

Colby simply stared at Dondell and thought: That man is going to kill me.

Meeker was feeling rounds erupting into him already.

None of them thought about God.

Stocker, too, like Vogt, was trembling, but for a different reason. He gazed at the bunch of men in front of him and his mouth became wet, as though someone had just presented him with his favourite dish, hot and steaming, and smelling so rich. The corners of his mouth twitched.

'Get your clothes off,' he said in a low, clogged voice.

There was a moment's stunned silence, then Garrett snarled, '*Shove it*! *Asshole*!'

From the chopper came Endean's voice.

'What about this guy?'

In the pilot's area, Marco was lounging back in his seat, trying to look as relaxed as one can look when every nerve-end, every tissue-fibre is electric with tension. He was slumped sideways, his right arm over the back of his seat, and his left hand resting on top of his hold-all. He saw Endean, who was now standing beside him, flick a glance over his right shoulder as he called out. It was all that

Marco needed.

Smoothly his fingers flicked open the hold-all and pulled out the automatic snugly buried there. His arm came right round in a fast arc.

'Eat lead, cocksucker,' he said, squeezing the trigger.

The bullet, like all those in the magazine, was soft-nosed and crossed. Marco had prepared them specially. It took Endean in the throat and went straight up into his chin and on, taking the top of his head away and paint-spraying the roof of the cabin with blood and brains. Convulsively, Endean's finger jerked at the trigger of the M-16 as he was punched backwards, and a long burst of automatic fire hammered across the instrument panel and Marco's seat.

But Marco was long gone, even in that split-second. His door was open and he was in the air in a curving dive for the grass.

Stocker screamed. 'Cover them!' as he pulled out a grenade and hurled it at the chopper. It flew in through the port door at an angle and detonated at the height of its parabola, near the roof of the pilot's area. Glass and aluminium bloomed outwards and the whole machine rocked violently up on its nose then back down again with a solid crash.

Marco, in the grass, was moving at the sprint, in a line away from and then round the shuddering chopper. His gun barked once, and the bullet exploded into the top of Dondell's helmet, jerking him off his feet and half-throttling him as the strap bit into his throat.

Garrett jumped forward and sank his left boot into McGerr's groin. McGerr gave a thin scream and doubled up, and Garrett put the other boot into his jaw. Olsen kicked Stocker's legs from under him and caught him as he fell, throwing an arm-lock round his throat and snapping his head back.

Marco stopped running. It was over.

He stooped and picked up Stocker's Armalite, then he walked over to Meeker, who was sitting on the ground with his head in his hands. As the tall black's shadow fell over him Meeker looked up, then cringed back, one arm raised to ward off any kick or blow that might be coming his way.

'Relax,' said Marco cheerfully. 'You may be a shithead, Meeker, but you sure as hell pulled our nuts outta the vise.' He grinned. 'See, ever since our little tête-à-tête, way back, I been prepared. I mean, *I* know lightnin' never strikes twice in the same fuckin' place, but does God? You answer that question correctly, Meeker, an' you jus' might get to open the box.'

He strolled over to where Olsen was covering Stocker with an M-16. Stocker was lying on the ground like a fallen statue, tensed and with his fingers digging into the earth. His face was white, and his breath came in short, shallow heaves. He didn't look at Marco.

'Hi, Stock,' said Marco amiably. Then he bent over the man, and said softly, 'Stocker, you a pig-fucker. You a pig-fucker of the first water. An' you gonna spill the beans or I'm gonna spill your guts.'

Stocker said nothing. He was trembling now, shaking quite violently. There was an expression of pure animal rage on his face. His eyes met Marco's and he spat up at him.

Marco carefully wiped the blob of spittle off his cheek and stood up. He kicked Stocker casually but firmly in the face, opening up the skin under his right eye. Stocker made no sound.

'You want to kick the basstud harder than that,' growled Garrett. 'I'd take the fucker's eyes out. In fact, that's exactly what I'm gonna do right now.'

'Leave it,' said Marco sharply. 'What's your rank?'

Garrett looked puzzled.

'Guess I don't have one. I got busted for killing a dink.'

Marco jerked a thumb at Olsen and moved away from the little group.

'You tell me, baby—name, rank, and orders?'

Olsen shrugged.

'Olsen, and Christ knows what I am out here. Was a sergeant, but I killed my lieutenant. They pulled me out of the stockade for this—like these others—some kind of rescue op, they said. But it seems to me they were gonna kill us anyway, unless that Stocker is just a crazy man. He looks like it.'

'Hoo-ee,' breathed Marco. 'This one, it stinks. It stinks

outrageous. You kill your Loot, that big guy kills a dink, an' young Stocker, he jus' a big ole mess. You is all jail-birds, baby, pulled out of the slammer for reasons unknown.' He indicated the others. 'Name 'em off.'

Olsen did so, and Marco ran his eyes over them, judging their potential. It was not very great. Meeker was useless, Garrett looked to be a trouble-maker, O'Mara and Vogt looked sick as dogs, and Colby didn't look like he had his head together. Olsen seemed solid, and maybe the medic, Pepper—Jesus, *Doctor* Pepper! It *had* to be!—was cool.

'What about the Huey?' Olsen was saying. 'Maybe we can fly out of here, Captain?'

'No way. Don't even need to look at it, Sarge. You get a frag grenade in a confined space, it don't stay confined very long. No controls, no radio—no shit.'

Olsen said, 'Vogt was given a radio, and there's a pile of Armalites in a crate at the back. We had plenty of clips.'

'Check 'em out.' He called to Vogt. 'Go get your radio, man. Get us some contact with the outside world.'

He walked across to McGerr.

'Ain't gonna waste time with you, baby. You jus' tell me the story, right?'

McGerr was still holding himself and groaning. He looked up, grey-faced and sweating.

'Okay, okay. I don't know nothin', Captain. All I was told, we was gonna ferry these guys out to Laos then shoot 'em. There was something about a rescue op—some guy called Hardin. That's what they were told. Stocker and the rest of us were gonna dump the chopper, trek east to a Laotian ville, pick up a cache, and head back over the border. We had to make sure this Hardin character was nailed, but you saw that chopper smash back there. He's had it, for sure.' He winced and moved his hand gently across his groin. 'An' that's the story. That's it. That's all I know.'

'A sweet tale, scumbag, you know it.' He turned and yelled to Vogt. 'What's with the aetherial mutterings, son?'

'Sorry, sir?'

'Jesus, the level of education in this man's army. You get to know more in the fuckin' ghetto, an' ain't that the truth. You made contact yet?'

119

'Uh . . . nossir.'

'What you gettin'?'

'Nothing, sir.'

'Open it up an' you tell me jus' what hits you straight between the eyes when you look inside, Vogt.'

'Yessir.' Vogt opened out the radio, blinked at it in puzzlement. 'Uh . . . sir. There don't seem to be any batteries, sir.'

'Figures.'

Marco had a strong feeling that he was being pulled down deep into some very spooky shit. This had all the hallmarks of a clandestine hit, but whether it was official or not he couldn't begin to imagine. All he knew was that they were stuck in Laos and they had to haul ass back to Nam damn fast, or all kinds of crap would be flying their way.

He knew Hardin vaguely; had ferried him once or twice into Cambodia. Why anyone should want to knock him off was beyond him for the moment, even if what McGerr had said were true, and he didn't intend to pursue the matter. There was too much else to think about.

Stocker had mentioned this ville, Mek Lonh, and so had McGerr. If it was a Special Forces hang-out, could be they might bump into some Green Berets there. Or Nungs working the area. Whatever. And there was a cache there, too.

He beckoned to Olsen.

'Tie Stocker an' the other dudes together. Rope round the neck. Wire, if you can find it. Get the portables together—food, ammunition, guns—make up packs. We movin' out. Try and find this ville.' He touched the big man on the arm. 'Far as I'm concerned, you still a sarge—okay, Sarge? You a real Papa Sierra. So get it on.'

Stocker's eyes followed Marco as the black moved around near the chopper. Into his mind leapt a vision of the Tun Phouc ditch, and he saw red against white and black against red: rivulets of blood oozing sluggishly out of torn flesh, and flies descending in little clouds to buzz and feast. A nerve throbbed at the corner of his right eye. He began to chuckle quietly to himself.

VII

Holding the Kalashnikov loosely in his right hand, Hardin emerged from the bushes and walked at an easy, unhurried pace into the hamlet's central square, as though he was strolling into the main shopping plaza back home in Montpelier, Vermont.

Yet his nerves were tense, screwed up. He was ready to explode into violent action at the slightest unnatural movement.

In the end, despite his hunger, he'd extended his own personal deadline by yet another half-hour, and, all told, had watched the ville for one hour and 45 minutes. He wasn't quite sure why he'd done this, except that however secure the place looked to be on the surface, however laid-back the atmosphere, still he had a gut-feeling that something was amiss. Or, if not exactly amiss, not entirely in order.

But he couldn't put his finger on what it was, and in the end had rationalised the feeling simply by pointing out to himself that maybe he was getting too paranoid about the overall situation. Hatred of Dempsey was colouring his attitude to everything. He was seeing the fat bastard's influence everywhere, and that was making him over-cautious. which was just as much of a fatal mistake as being not cautious enough.

He headed straight for the headman's hut and as he moved he was relieved to see that the mama-sans didn't suddenly grab for their children, or do more than glance up at him for a couple of seconds before going back to whatever chores they were engaged in.

The men turned their heads towards him, but incuriously, as though they had seen such a sight many times before. Which they undoubtedly had. No one made any sudden or hostile moves.

The old woman on the steps of the headman's hut opened her eyes, took in the scene, then called back over her shoulder. As Hardin nodded casually to her and began to mount the steps, the headman emerged from the open door, blinking his eyes against the sun. He smiled, held out his hand.

'Welcome,' he said in perfect English. 'You are an honoured and welcome visitor. You will accept the humble hospitality of my poor village.'

That was a formula; he probably said it to everyone who came, whether they were Green Berets, NVA, of the Pathet Lao. It was true that there were many villages in Indo China which were solidly for one guerilla organisation, and solidly against another. But most trod a delicate path between the various political ideologies, and, on the surface, were friendly to all. It paid, in the long run.

Hardin shook his hand. The man was in his mid-50s, solidly-built, and clearly capable of looking after himself and his village. His smile extended to his eyes, though that was no guarantee that he wasn't about to set Hardin up in some way or other.

'I accept your hospitality with great pleasure,' said Hardin, thinking, as he invariably did on such occasions, that all this was exactly like some stately, formal 18th century dance—a gavotte, say, where the steps and intricate formations were set down precisely, and you followed them no matter what.

'Tell your people I mean them no harm,' he went on, 'and that my friendship is assured.'

The headman nodded.

'You will be here for a long time?'

'I will be here for as long as I will be here,' said Hardin. 'But probably for at least three days.'

In fact, he had no intention of staying for more than 18 hours at the outside. He wanted to be away just before dawn the next day, but it did no harm to let the headman think otherwise. If he was to be set up in some kind of trap, the headman would think he had plenty of time to spring it, and would thus be slow to alert any hostile forces that might be in the vicinity.

'You are alone,' asked the headman.

'Others will be here,' said Hardin without hesitation. He pulled out his cigarettes and offered the pack. The headman took one and Hardin lit it for him. They sat down on chairs that had been brought up by a young boy,

122

probably one of the headman's sons, and drank mint tea from small bowls. It was all very civilised.

'Have you had any NVA or Pathet Lao forces through here recently?'

The headman shrugged.

'We keep ourselves to ourselves,' he said conventionally. 'Americans come and go always. Many of them. Some in groups, others like you, alone.' He glanced at Hardin. 'Some with supplies, others without.'

Hardin noticed that the headman hadn't answered his original question, but in a way, such was the precarious nature of the villagers' existence and the philosophy of caution that continually ordered their lives, that was only to be expected. The sly hint about supplies was normal too. The headman wanted to know if Hardin knew about the cache that had been prepared somewhere around here.

'Supplies,' repeated Hardin, nodding. 'We will see about those before I leave.'

Actually, he intended to plunder the cache tomorrow morning, on the way out. Just to be on the safe side he could do with more medical supplies, and, more importantly, clothes. He had no doubt at all that the cache, whatever size it was, would have a supply of hard-wearing jungle fatigues in it.

He looked out on the square, smoking casually, sipping his tea, his legs out in front of him: a picture, he knew, of almost indolent ease. As if he hadn't a worry in the world.

Noon came and went; the day stretched itself sleepily into late afternoon. Hardin oiled and cleaned his AK-47 and the two automatics. He stripped down and bathed in a large wooden tub in an outlying shed, the rifle primed and lying on a box near him. His clothes, soaped and scrubbed and thumped by a fat mama-san, dried off in the afternoon sun while he lounged at the corner of the headman's verandah, clad in a soft linen loincloth, smoking, his eyes never leaving the village square for more than a few moments at a time.

Soon the shadows from the tall trees to the west of the hamlet began to lengthen, lapping slowly but inexorably over the thatched-roof huts, and a refreshingly cool breeze sprang up, wiping away the stickiness of the day. Hardin dressed and waited for food. He was offered a pipe of opium, but politely refused it.

Not that he was averse to the drug; quite the contrary. The odd pipe suited him well enough, but he'd had his share of 'chasing the dragon'—and, on occasion, of being chased by dragons; some particularly ugly and repulsive breeds of the phantom creature.

There were two main types in the US forces over here in Vietnam: heads and boozers. Heads smoked and boozers drank. It so happened that Hardin had found himself, strangely for a man over the age of 30, in the heads' camp, simply because as a teenager in the early 1950s, he'd bummed around the States, drifted to San Francisco, and hung around with the early Beats on the waterfront. His idols in those days had been jazzmen, of just about any denomination. He had Catholic tastes; could take Lu Watters as well as Clifford Brown or Art Pepper. He'd listened to Parker blowing like an angel after-hours; had caught Fats Navarro in New York just before the fat man died, a shrivelled husk of a heroin addict but still making his horn sing sweetly.

Hardin had tried the hard stuff, but death put him off it: he saw the grim effects it had on too many guys he respected. He read up on the subject, mainly the literature of the soft stuff, from Thomas de Quincey, through Fitz Hugh Ludlow's *The Hasheesh Eater*, to Mezz Mezzrow, and it was the latter, with his picaresque tales of making a buck by peddling marijuana on street corners in Harlem in the 1930s, when his clarinet was in hock, who could be said to have truly turned him on.

Not that he hit it now all that often, but when he did—the occasional comradely pipe with Jean Ottavj, the Corsican proprietor of the Royal Hotel in Nguyen Thiep Street and a noted Saigon character—it was with pleasure, and in the knowledge that he was delivering a solid and damaging kick to the system which, in the Army, said that when you relaxed the way to do it was to get blind hooting drunk, the way men of violence should. This man of violence, thought Hardin, sought only dreamy peace.

He ate with the headman: chunky meat stew with blood-thickened gravy, a rice dish with bean shoots, cheese and fresh guavas. More mint tea was brought, refreshing and fragrant. Hardin smoked and thought about Dempsey.

It was clear that Dempsey had been behind the bomb in the chopper; equally clear that it was Dempsey who'd been pulling strings so that he should be jumping up and down the length and breadth of Vietnam and not knowing what the hell was going on.

Hardin acknowledged that he himself had made a mistake in not blowing the whistle on Dempsey boo-coo fast. On the other hand a great deal of the evidence he had against him was personal knowledge, but undocumented. The fact that Dempsey owned, or at least had some sort of a finger in, local brothels, hotels, bars and the like, was, as Dempsey himself had pointed out, chicken-shit. Such involvements were not uncommon, natural perquisites for crusaders far from home.

With the Tun Phouc massacre Hardin was possibly on firmer ground. He knew that Dempsey had personally ordered the killings—to encourage the others, as it were—and he knew that the main participant in the blood-letting had been a Sergeant Alvin Stocker, who had then been pulled off active combat duty and given a safe posting in Saigon. Still, with the My Lai shit flying back in the World, he had to admit he wasn't entirely certain how Command would view yet another, and far worse, scandal hitting the headlines. It was on the cards that those higher up the tree than Dempsey might go out of their way to squash all knowledge of it slipping out too. That they might frown on Dempsey, but side with him. That they might decide to protect their own.

Dempsey's dealings with Vietnamese politicos, however, were a whole set of different ball-games—still undocumented, it was true, but stone-cold factual, and capable of being dug up with ease by anyone sufficiently interested in, or alarmed by, their implications.

Hardin had several names, but the chief one was a man called Nguen Ton Chi, a powerful but somewhat shadowy figure who had links with Buddhist activists and other radicals inimical to the governing Thieu regime. These links were, however, far more tenuous, Hardin had discovered, than the links Chi had, oblique as these were in their turn, with men who had a more or less direct line to the North Vietnamese government in Hanoi. And that was dynamite.

The trouble was, it was difficult, in this morally ambiguous conflict, to retain any sense of what was right and what was wrong. Political expedience often meant sleeping with strange bed-fellows: siding with the wolf to destroy the tiger one week, then resuscitating the tiger the next, to pull down the wolf.

Hardin knew, for instance, that the Pepsi-Cola bottling plant in Vientiane, dedicated by Nixon before he made it to the Presidency, was the largest factory manufacturing heroin in the whole of South East Asia. He knew too (it was an open secret) that Air America in Vietnam was CIA-controlled, but he also knew that the CIA used Air America to run the heroin all over the Asian sub-continent.

Faced with facts like these, and others even more sinister and outrageous, it became almost impossible to make any sort of moral judgement on the conflict that was ripping South East Asia apart, and just as impossible to view the actions of those who were in charge of the conduct of the Vietnam war in particular with anything other than alarm and despondency.

Hardin acknowledged to himself that by involving himself in politics he'd committed a monumental mistake. He should've stayed in the jungle. But once he'd started to find out about Dempsey, he'd started to discover other, and far more appalling, secrets about other people and other organisations. It had been difficult to know where to stop, yet all he'd wanted in the first place was a weapon with which to threaten Dempsey should he ever prove too demanding. Dempsey had a habit of corrupting those closest to him, even by implication, and Hardin had wanted none of it. Now, for Christ's sake, he was up to his neck.

On the other hand maybe he'd got it wrong? Maybe Dempsey's strange ties were official policy, part of some complex and devious strategy worked out at the highest level?

And then he saw Dempsey's face in his mind, as he'd last seen it in the room in the hotel off Tu Do, and he thought about the bomb in the chopper that had destroyed three people.

No, this was Dempsey's private can of worms and Dempsey could not afford for him to come out of the jungle alive. Dempsey, the fat rat, was gunning for him for real.

The hell with him, thought Hardin. I'll nail the fucker to the front door of his Goddamn hotel, string him up to his crystal chandeliers. I'll *waste* him.

He lit another cigarette and wondered when the headman would get around to offering him, in the circuitous way this was normally done, a woman. The thought triggered a pulse in him, that became a slow, warm sensation that drifted lazily through his groin. He glanced at the headman, and the impulse vanished as swiftly as it had manifested itself, as though he had dipped himself in a bucket of crushed ice.

Standing in the doorway to one side of the headman, in full uniform that included the slightly absurd solar topee worn on almost every occasion, was an officer in the North Vietnamese Army.

Hardin froze. The fact that he did not drop his right hand from the table the foot or so it needed to grab the AK-47 placed in readiness at his side and start blasting was no reflection on either his courage or his natural speed of manoeuvre. On the contrary, it said a lot for his presence of mind in a situation where most men would have panicked.

Because no way was he going to be able to beat the levelled assault rifles held by the two NVA regulars flanking the officer, pointing straight at him.

But even though he stayed exactly where he was, making absolutely no move that could be interpreted even loosely as a hostile action, his mind was racing.

Because the man standing in the doorway was not just an officer. He was a very senior officer. Goddamnit, he was a *thieu tuong*, the NVA equivalent of a major-general.

Incredibly, the man smiled, nodded amiably at Hardin. He stepped into the room casually, as though he was just a neighbour dropping in for a smoke and a drink and a gossip about the day's events.

The headman stood up, bowed to the Vietnamese, bowed to Hardin, and then gestured to his family. They all

127

filed out.

The *thieu tuong* took off his hat, and held out his hand.

'How do you do.'

Hardin, for want of anything better to do, shook the proffered hand. The *thieu tuong* turned and snapped his fingers. A junior officer came through the door holding two glass tumblers and a bottle of wine, which he proceeded to open. Hardin stared at the label. It was a 1962 Margaux, chateau bottled. He wondered if he was dreaming all this, if maybe he'd actually taken some opium sometime in the past hour or so without noticing.

The *thieu tuong* swirled a measure of the wine round in his tumbler, sniffed it, and drank. He smiled again.

'1962,' he said, 'a good year.'

'Hell of a good year,' agreed Hardin, 'one of the best.'

'One of my colleagues in Paris,' said the *thieu tuong*, 'prefers the Lafite.'

'Very good,' nodded Hardin, 'but not the same.'

'Ah, a man of discrimination, of discernment. That is excellent. So much more civilised to do business with a man of taste.'

The junior officer poured the wine and Hardin swirled it in his glass, releasing the full nutty bouquet. He took some in, let it wash around his mouth, smacked his lips appreciatively.

'Hell of a year,' he murmured.

'Splendid.' The *thieu tuong* sat down across the table from him. 'My name is Hoang Van Tho,' he said. 'I believe you have something for me.'

PART THREE

I

'I don't like it,' said Doc Pepper. 'It . . . it's too quiet, man.'

'No way is your sense of humour appreciated by this dude,' said Marco. 'Fact is, boy, this dude says you jus' shut yo' honky mouth.' He stared down at the village. 'Although I'll allow there might be a particle of truth lurking down there in what you say. Just a Goddamn particle.'

From their vantage point overlooking the village's central square they could see nothing that moved, except the leaping, dancing flames of the two big fires at each end. All, except one, of the huts were in darkness; the exception was a bigger hut with a verandah at the top of the square, where light could just be seen around loose window-hangings. The only sounds that broke the night-silence were the occasional bullet-like cracks of bursting wood on one or other of the fires, and the low, persistent sawing of cicadas nearby.

'They go to bed early round here,' said Doc Pepper.

'Work hard, sweat hard, sleep hard,' said Marco. 'Ain't they got fun.' He half-turned his head. 'Hey, Sarge.'

Olsen wriggled up silently behind them, and slid in beside Marco on top of the knoll.

'Pepper, here, he don't like it,' whispered Marco. 'And to tell the truth, Sarge, no more do I. It's really kind of early for these dudes to be racked down.'

Olsen stared at the scene, remembering past attacks on villages at night. There weren't even any dogs to be seen here, let alone the odd human figure mooching about. He glanced at his watch.

'Well, maybe, Captain. You would maybe think there ought to be more movement, sure, but they frankly don't have much to do after nightfall.'

'Affirm on that, Sarge. I mean, no movies, bowling alleys, floodlit Goddamn baseball. But it still don't smell right.'

'There's light up there—looks like the honcho's hut.'

'Yeah, an' that ain't cool, either. Like they all in there, doin' all them secretive magical rites, maybe. Forget it.'

Olsen stuck his elbows out, laid his hands, palms down, flat on the grass, and rested his chin on them. He peered intently at the deeper darkness between two huts across the square below, opening his eyes wide and consciously attempting to swivel his eyeballs away from each other. That was impossible, of course, but the action sharpened the focus. He grunted quietly; it was almost a chuckle. He shifted his position, focused on other gaps.

'There are men down there,' he muttered to Marco. 'In the shadows between the huts, out of the firelight.'

Marco stared, wincing in concentration.

'Damn,' he said softly. 'Dig it, they got them sun-hats on, too. They Goddamn EnVees. Je-sus. They'd've blown our shit away, sure enough.'

'I guess it's some kind of trap,' said Olsen.

'Who for? Us? Christ, Sarge, them mothers they don't even know we exist. At least,' he amended, remembering the vibes he'd had on the LZ earlier, 'I don't think they know we exist. No, wait on. Damn right they don't know we exist. We supposed to be blown away by Stocker hours ago.'

'So it's a trap for Stocker and the others?' said Doc Pepper.

'Shee-it, how in hell do I know?' complained Marco. 'This caper is damn complicated enough, without you throwin' in all this brain-teasin' shit.'

He was beginning to feel irritable. It was bad enough being hijacked a second time (no one was going to be very happy about that back at Base), then losing a chopper, then getting saddled with a bunch of misfits, murderers and Goddamn no-hopers and having to trek through the jungle in the noonday sun, without all this extra spooky shit dumped down on him.

'Whoever they waitin' for, ain't gonna be us walks into their damn lines of fire.'

Light suddenly streamed across the verandah of the headman's hut, as a window-hanging fell away from the window. Figures could be seen inside the room; some kind of struggle appeared to be in progress. Marco could make out the figures quite clearly before the hanging was thrust back into place, cutting off his view and the square of yellow light.

'Holy Christ,' he said wonderingly. 'That was Hardin in there, the dude that's supposed to be a burnt-out case back in that chopper crash. So what in hell he doin' here?'

'Man, it looked like they were having some tussle in there,' said Doc Pepper. 'Some tough tussle.'

'So you've read Ambrose Bierce, baby,' said Marco sourly. 'So you think you can throw quotes at me, boy. So I think you a salty little shit, Doc Pepper, an' you better close down your station, 'fore I close it down for you.' He swivelled his head to Olsen. 'You got Colby, Vogt and O'Mara thrown out on our perimeters?'

'Yessir.'

'An' that badmouth Garrett watchin' Stocker and his bunch of shit?'

'And watching Meeker, too, sir. I've taken Meeker's gun away from him. Seemed the best move to make. He's frankly been acting in a very weird kind of way since we started, sir.'

'That's cool. He ain't no badass, he a Goddamn *madass*.' Marco pondered the situation for a couple of seconds, no longer. 'Okay, Pepper, you keep a look out here. Any movement in our direction, you tell the sarge.' He tapped Olsen's shoulder. 'You take over from Garrett. I got plans for him. Those four dudes act up, ice 'em.'

'With all respect, sir, I figure, should the crap really get to flying, we're gonna need all the firepower we can muster, sir.'

'Meeker,' said Marco, 'does not—repeat not, Sarge—get a gun. No damn way. An' nor does Stocker.'

'Roger that, sir. I mean, I think there is something seriously wrong with Stocker's head. The way he was laughing, even when he had the rope collar on and we were heading through the jungle—well, Jesus, sir. I really don't know what it is with him, but, dammit, I got a feeling he's way over the top. Deranged, sir. You know?'

'Out to lunch, Sarge.'

'But the other two, sir—Dondell and McGerr. In a heavy situation, sir, I think we're frankly gonna have to trust 'em.'

131

There was still no movement below. The two fires were not burning so fiercely now, and the darkness seemed thicker and blacker, almost substantial; something you could reach out and touch. Marco stared at the village moodily and thought: ain't this a yell?

He said, 'Garrett and me, we do a recon. Close recon. See what the fuck is doin' down there. We don't appear in two hours, get the hell out, Sarge. Gather 'em up, and fade. All you do is keep movin' east till you reach the border.'

They slid silently into the trees and down the other side of the knoll to where Garrett could just be seen in the gloom, sitting against a tree, his M-16 leaning against his raised knees. Opposite him Stocker and the two gunners were tied to a tree, and Meeker was lying on the ground, staring apathetically up into the night.

'You got a knife, Garrett?'

The big man looked up, grinning.

'Nossir.'

'Sarge, you picked one up out of the chopper. Give it to Garrett.'

Garrett kept on grinning. He held something up in his hand.

'Don't need no knife, Captain. Got me this. Been whipping it into shape just now. Only got two wires, and I prefer four, and it ain't piano wire either. But what the hell.'

Marco peered down at the object.

'You can use it?'

'Slice right through to the fucking vertebrae with it. Begging your pardon, Captain.'

Marco grinned too. This he could deal with. He bent over Garrett.

'You an' me, we gonna get on fine. Garrett, long as you don't hold out any hopes of usin' this cheese-slicer on me. Raised in Harlem, baby.' He patted the knife-sheath at his belt. 'My speed is unnatural.'

'Is that right, Captain?'

'It was said that Lucifer, Prince of Darkness, had a hand in my begettin'.'

'I'll remember that, Captain.'

'Do.' Marco turned and muttered to Olsen, 'Re Dondell

and McGerr, Sarge, you do what you think necessary.' He beckoned to Garrett. 'Let's move, soldier.'

It took them a half hour to reach Marco's objective, the rear of the ville. They threaded their way silently through the gloom of the jungle, moving across damp grass and soggy earth, and keeping as far as possible away from any surface that seemed treacherously dry. It was slow work, using your hands to feel ahead for dead branches that might snap loudly and crash to the ground or creepers that could tangle you up and throw you off-balance. Unseen creatures slithered and skittered by; the incessant sawing of the cicadas jammed out other sounds and twisted the nerves.

Marco disliked the jungle. Fly-boys usually did. Up there, in the sky, even if you were in a tiny Loach with the cabin area pressing you tight and the plexiglass roof almost touching your head, you were still free. Like they said, free as a bird. You could sweep and spiral and zoom and soar, and get the hell out fast if danger threatened. Down here you had no chance. It was an alien landscape teeming with alien perils, and most of them concealed, invisible until the last moment. Especially in the dark. You had absolutely no idea what was dropping down on you from above, or what you were putting your boot into, or if the smooth leafless branch you brushed away from you might suddenly strike back at you and bury poison-tipped fangs into your arm. And no way could you get the hell out fast.

Garrett shifted his way under the huge leathery fronds of some unseen tree, his eyes flicking to left and right expertly. His night-vision was good—always had been— and the jungle consequently held no terrors for him. Shapes swam into his line of vision and were instantly, and correctly, identified: boles of trees, shrubs, a thick tangle of vegetation to be skirted, creepers as thick as your arm that hung down singly, or were plaited with others into a leafy network that could be brushed aside with ease, and in silence.

He was still in two minds about this whole crazy business. He could either stick with the nigger, or simply and suddenly—right now, in fact—branch off at a tangent and make it to the border on his own. Leave the rest of

133

them here. Jesus Christ, they were definitely the sickest bunch of fuckers he'd ever seen. How in hell could they ever make it back in one piece through bandit country with a couple (at least) of scared and useless kids and a couple (at least) of fucking madmen on the roster?

No, his best plan was to light out fast; search out and join up with one of those gangs of marauders—deserters for the most part—working the jungle up in the north. He'd heard there were good pickings to be had from some of those villes up in the Highlands. Or maybe strike south down into Cambodia. Or maybe even slough off his identity entirely and work his way back into Nam from the west and lose himself in Saigon. It was a big city. He had good contacts there and in any case he still had some unfinished business that had to be cleared away. He could move in with one of the gangs that worked the docks.

On the other hand, doing that would mean he would not be able to waste Stocker, and that was a pleasure he'd promised himself, nailing that crazy bastard.

Could be there was someone bigger behind Stocker; probably was (that Special Forces captain, for instance)— but Stocker was the man on the spot, and Stocker was gonna get it. As far as he was concerned, Stocker had dropped him in this shit (and the fact that Stocker had also, by implication, hauled him out of the slammer, made no difference at all: it was the present that counted) and Stocker had to die. *Then* get back to Saigon and fix that double-crossing dink Ngo Van Toan. It was a matter of professional pride.

Garrett came to a sudden halt. His questing eyes had caught a movement that didn't fit in with the kind of movement he was used to in this environment; an alien shape where no shape ought to be.

He was in deep shadow. He knew, because it was instinctive in him to fix himself in such a position, that if he moved now there would be no tell-tale dark silhouette against a lighter background. He sank silently into a squatting position, and began to orientate himself, breathing quietly through his mouth.

The undergrowth was thinning out here; he could see that he was very near to their objective, the hut Marco had told him about, with light seeping out of cracks and chinks in the frame. He saw that he was almost behind this large hut; about ten yards to one side of it. In between were trees, and it was against one of these that . . .

A feral smile touched his lips: the smile of the hunter. The shape had been a man, with a topee on his head, shifting his position under one of the trees—just like he was doing again right now. Maybe he wanted to take a leak, maybe he was just cramped. Whatever, it was gonna be the death of him, thought Garrett.

He rose to a standing position, unfastening the wire and toggles from a hook on his fatigues. He wondered where Marco was. Long as the nigger didn't start thrashing around suddenly, this guy was easy meat. Jesus Christ, he wasn't even holding his rifle. *Very* careless.

Garrett slid forward like a cat through the gloom, his boots making no sound at all on the lightly moist ground. Now he was five yards from his target; now three. His eyes took in his immediate surroundings, noted that the slope's hat was strapped (better and better!), then ranged further away. Nothing. Unless the number suddenly shifted again, he was a dead man.

He raised his hands, the wire hanging slack between them, then with a swift, smooth motion, taking care to swing it out that extra inch or so to avoid snagging on the brim of the hat, he dropped it over the man's head, cross-toggled and pulled.

The man's body arched in agony, his head jerking back but the helmet holding firm because of the strap. Then the body slumped. Garrett bent his elbows, straining, holding the dead weight up by main force. The stench of loosened bowels hit his nostrils, but he paid no attention. He began to lower the body gently to the ground, keeping it away from him, very slowly, even though pain was flowing through the muscles in his arms.

'A clean kill,' came Marco's voice softly from behind him.

'The way I like it,' he muttered.

Marco pointed through the trees at the hut, at the narrow alleyway dividing the bigger building from its neighbours. He put his mouth to Garrett's ear.

'Two in there, nearer us than the front. You take the first

one. Bring him to you.'

He watched as Garrett faded into the darkness and then cat-footed through the trees until he was beside the structure. His knife was already in his hand. He eased himself towards the gap then flattened himself against the wooden wall.

Garrett appeared on the other side of the gap, holding his Armalite. He stood the weapon on its butt, then let it go. The rifle fell to the ground with a muffled thump, and even as it did so Garrett had disappeared again into the shadows.

Tensed, his head turned sideways and resting lightly against the wall, Marco kept quite still as an EnVee suddenly appeared from out of the alleyway, peering round the other corner, his back turned towards him. It made a good and solid target, but was not, as far as Marco was concerned, the object of the present exercise.

The EnVee went right round to the back of the other hut, stopping as he noticed the rifle on the grass. Garrett came out of the shadows swiftly. Neither he nor the EnVee made any sound whatsoever, but suddenly the EnVee was a huddled shape on the ground. Marco grinned as Garrett took his helmet off and placed the dead man's topee on his head. He crouched down, inching forward so that the hat was now just to be seen in the mouth of the alley.

Another figure came into view, stooping too, and Marco stepped forward fast, throwing his left arm round the guy's head and pulling it back. His knife slid into and cross the throat, and blood pumped hotly and stickily over his hands.

They shifted the bodies into the trees, then moved back to the hut. All was silent; not even a night-bird croaked.

'Far as I can tell,' whispered Marco, 'it's all happening in the central room.'

'Door at the back of the building?'

'Uh-uh. Checked it out. Flat wall.'

'So, if we wanna get in, we have to mount the front steps and walk in through the front door? With all them slopes watching from the square? Smart thinking, Captain.'

'Don't crap me, Garrett. We go *under* the hut.' Marco tugged at the man's sleeve and squatted down, pointing at

136

the wide gap under the building. 'Built on piles. We gonna slide in. You gonna watch the square from underneath, so you jus' keep your eyes peeled, soldier. Keep them orbs *eager*.'

II

Hoang Van Tho said, 'This is absurd, Colonel. I thought you were a sensible man. Why do you not give me what I want?'

Hardin gazed at the man through blurred eyes, trying hard to concentrate. If he did not concentrate, if he let himself sink back into luxurious unconsciousness, they would only bring him out of it again, cause more pain and damage.

His ears were ringing where he'd been clubbed repeatedly about the head with rifle-butts, there were several cigarette burns on his chest, his face was bruised and one eye was half-closed. His head ached intolerably, right behind the eyes, the worst possible place. The knuckles of his right hand were skinned too, but that was a minor grazing and was not in fact attributable to Tho or his men—at least not directly. That was where he'd landed badly at the beginning of the session after he'd tried to escape and had been flung across the room by one of the regulars.

He thought that Tho had hit the nail on the head. Right crack in the centre. It *was* absurd. *Truly* absurd. Because, in the beginning, realising that he had nothing to gain—or even, such was his position, nothing to lose—by not telling the truth, he'd told it.

'I don't have anything for you,' he'd said, and Tho had laughed as though at a mildly amusing joke and offered him more wine. It struck Hardin instantly that not only did Tho not believe him, but he obviously thought he was merely playing safe, or holding out for some kind of extra delivery charge.

Because that was it: that was the key-word—delivery. All this was about the packet Dempsey had originally wanted him to deliver. 'A drop in the ville, nothing big deal,' was how he'd put it. 'To oblige the spooks.'

Well, Hardin had long since figured out that this drop wasn't a regular CIA operation; that the only person to be obliged was Dempsey himself. And he'd figured out too that the deal was a dirty one, a real bottom-drawer, under-the-counter effort. What hadn't occurred to him for one moment was that it was to be as dirty as this; a straight hand-over to a high-ranking member of the NVA Command. Which meant that whatever it was in that packet – and he'd originally assumed that it might have something to do with drugs, of one kind or another, or some pay-off Dempsey needed to make in a hurry – was so hot as to be incandescent. Hell, this was a simple case of trafficking with the Goddamn enemy.

But all that was beside the point, which was that he was now in very deep shit whichever way you looked at it. Because even if he'd had the packet, no doubt Tho, after finishing the wine with him, would have shot him out of hand. You didn't leave witnesses to a deal like this.

Not having the packet made it that much worse. Tho had expected a courier at such a time and in such a place, and— on time, on target—in had walked Hardin. The village headman must have been told to expect him, and probably figured everything was jake when Hardin moved in. Hardin remembered that the headman had expressed no surprise or horror when Tho had entered, and had bowed to them both before he'd left the room. Naturally. This was supposed to be a regular business deal after all. And now Tho wanted the goods, and was becoming more and more impatient at Hardin's tardiness in handing them over.

One thing was for sure: Tho would not appreciate the irony of the situation if Hardin explained matters in full. Hardin wasn't over the moon about it himself.

They'd finished off two glasses of wine when Hardin decided it was time to make a break for it. The door had been out of the question, so he'd shrugged his shoulders, said 'Okay, you can have the packet'—and jumped for the nearest window. The attempt had not been an unqualified success.

For a guy who understood the difference betwen a 1962 Margaux and a 1962 Lafite Tho was a fast mover. As Hardin had jumped, the Vietnamese had grabbed the bottle and heaved the table over, throwing Hardin off balance. He'd lost his momentum, lost the element of surprise. He'd made it to the window, but one of the regulars had reached there a quarter second later. The struggle had been violent but brief, Hardin losing interest in the proceedings for several minutes after a smashing blow to the back of his head.

He'd come round to find himself hunched in one of the chairs, naked to the waist, with his hands tied to one another under the chair-seat. Then the two regulars had started in on him, clubbing his face, burning him with cigarettes, beating him generally. The softening-up process.

Hardin soon realised that no way should he ever have given Tho the idea that he had the packet, because Tho now had it fixed firmly in his mind that Hardin had hidden it somewhere and was, for some obscure reason, holding out on him.

Now he repeated, 'Why do you not give me what I want? It's very simple. It was, after all, part of the original arrangement.'

'What arrangement?' said Hardin from deep down in his throat.

'Don't be stupid, Colonel. The arrangement between your principals and mine.'

'Dempsey is no Goddamn principal of mine.'

The Vietnamese breathed out irritably.

'Names mean nothing to me, Colonel. You must realise that, surely. You must also realise that I want that packet. You are really being excessively stupid, causing yourself unnecessary pain. Do you like pain? Do you gain pleasure from the infliction of pain on yourself? Is that the reason for this show of stubbornness?' He smiled as though slightly bewildered. 'I am quite prepared to give you much pain, much discomfort. But discomfort from which you will gain no pleasure whatsoever. On the other hand, were you to tell me where you have hidden the packet, we could finish that excellent bottle of wine, and part, if not friends, at least, ah . . . comrades? Comrades in arms? Yes?'

'Go to hell,' said Hardin. 'Even if I had the Goddamn packet, you'd still kill me.'

The Vietnamese stared at him silently for some moments. Then he turned to one of the regulars.

'Water.'

The regular went out of the room.

Tho lit a cigarette, using Hardin's lighter. He began to pace up and down the room, taking occasional sips of wine from his tumbler. He was, Hardin thought, in his late-40s, maybe early-50s. An intelligent man, who clearly kept himself fit, at the peak of condition.

Equally clearly he was a high-ranker, with far more influence even than his army rank implied. Political influence. His mention of Paris meant that he'd been, probably was still, on staff with Le Duc Tho round the table at the peace negotiations which had been dragging on now for over a year. So what in God's name was he doing here, in the wilds of Laos, acting as pick-up man? It didn't make any kind of sense to Hardin. Sure, he could imagine many items that Dempsey might have that would be of spectacular value to the North Vietnamese, but nothing that would pull a man like Hoang Van Tho nearly 7,000 miles to a tiny ville deep in the Laotian jungle.

The regular came back into the room, carrying two buckets of water. Tho gestured at Hardin, and the second regular jerked the chair backwards. Pain stabbed across Hardin's back and his wrists felt as though they'd been wrenched off his arms as the chair slammed down on to the floor.

'Very stupid,' said Tho.

One of the regulars sat on Hardin's chest, so that he could not move his legs. The EnVee pushed his head right back with one hand and forced his mouth open with the other. Hardin bit the man's fingers, sinking his teeth hard into the flesh just below the first joint, and grinding. He tasted blood. The man screamed and jabbed Hardin in the eye with his elbow. Hardin's head was jerked sideways and he grunted with pain.

Tho went to the door and shouted. Another regular came in.

'Very foolish,' sighed Tho.

Kneeling on Hardin's chest, the newcomer gripped his teeth and yanked his mouth open, almost splitting the corners. Hardin tried threshing around, jerking the man off him, but the weight on his cramped body was too much. He couldn't move. Through watering eyes he saw the third regular looming over him with the bucket. Water splashed down on to his face from the slopping pail, cooling his burning flesh, giving him, in an odd kind of way, a measure of relief. Then the man tipped the bucket slowly and carefully. As water poured down into Hardin's open mouth the man whose fingers he'd bitten reached down and pinched his nostrils closed.

Instantly he vomited, and the rising flood of bile met the steady stream of water in his throat, choking him. He couldn't move; it felt like he was squeezed tight in a vice, and no matter how hard he tried to struggle it didn't make any difference to the seemingly unending stream of liquid that filled his mouth and throat right down to his stomach. His air had all gone and panic washed over him in a dark, silently shrieking flood. He blacked out.

And came to as one of the regulars smacked his face lightly and repeatedly with his hand. He threw up again, vaguely aware that it was mostly water that was gushing out over his chin and chest.

Through a haze of pain and sickness he saw one of the Vietnamese pushing something down towards him, and his squeal of panic was cut off as a cloth was rammed into his mouth. He began to breathe frantically through his nose, pulling in air deeply and desperately, and then the black tide of horror raced through his mind again as water in a thinner stream entered his nostrils.

The back of his throat felt like it was on fire, felt as though flames blown by a gale of wind were searing up into his brain and down into his lungs. He thought Jesus I'm fucking drowning drowning fucking Jesus drowning—and blacked out again.

Repeated blows on the face woke him; his mouth was clear. He gulped in air raspingly. The grinning faces looking down at him were spinning slowly round and he vomited more water over himself, the motions much weaker now, and most of the liquid spilling over his chin and lower cheeks.

The faces above him parted and Tho's smiling features appeared, dipping down towards him.

'Finish your wine.'

Wine from the tumbler flooded his mouth, tasting

unbelievably harsh and bitter. Again his system reacted violently and he was sick, his body unrestrained by the weight of any of the Vietnamese, jerking in great stomach-wrenching, rib-cracking spasms.

'A pity to waste such a good vintage,' said Tho, his voice sounding as though he was throwing it from the other end of the village, 'but it was from your glass, Colonel. I would not have drunk it. I am particular, some might say fussy, about such matters. Pick him up.'

Hardin's head lolled to one side as the chair was heaved upright; he couldn't feel his hands now at all.

'Your wife,' said Tho, 'would not be pleased to see you in such a state. I understand that American women are somewhat fanatical about personal hygiene. Are you married, Colonel? Of course, you may not be. Perhaps you are one of those men who keep a Japanese lady happy in Okinawa. Where is the packet?'

Hardin said, 'Go to hell, shit-for-brains.'

At least, that was his intention. What actually emerged from his mouth were a number of mumbled, incomprehensible noises.

'Well,' said Tho decisively, 'we shall see. We shall see what we shall see when we attach wires from a generator to you.' He chuckled. 'You should be an interesting sight, Colonel, with all that water over you.'

He gestured at the buckets and two of the regulars picked them up and followed him out of the door, leaving Hardin alone with the one whose finger he'd bitten.

Hardin stared dully at the closed door. He was beginning to pull his mind back into shape. Nothing he could do about the burns, the bruises, or the fact that his stomach felt like someone had dug it out of him with an E-tool. Physical pain was shit when it was hitting you, but it didn't last forever.

The generator sounded like a bad deal, though. He knew the drill. They'd swab him down with more water, fix leads to his temples, then crank up. Well, that would add to the headache, jolt his brains round a little. Then they'd try a few other spots: his nipples, under his armpits (good place; plenty of moisture there, though that wouldn't matter so much with all the water they'd be throwing over him), palms of his hands. But he knew that this would simply be a big Goddamn tease, because what they'd be thinking about, and what he'd be thinking about, and what they'd know he'd be thinking about was the moment they decided to fix the wires to his dick.

Jesus, they'd have him jerking his groin higher than a hooker in a 42nd Street bump-and-grind.

There didn't seem to be any way out of this one. They were going to kill him very slowly and very painfully. Probably, at some stage or other, he was going to start talking, squawking louder than a parrot, telling Tho the whole story from A to Z. But that really wasn't going to help matters. Would merely make Tho madder, in fact. And the only thing that was going to save all this pain and mess was the arrival of the real courier. But Christ alone knew when he was going to turn up, and you could bet your last dollar he wouldn't be showing like the cavalry just when Tho was fixing up the generator leads.

His head was still throbbing abominably; so was his body. But his mind was beginning to sharpen up as he pummelled it into concrete thought, whipping it into creating sentences and silent consequential pictures. And while doing this, and taking his stock of surroundings, he was suddenly aware that his hands were loose. Not untied-loose, but in the sense that the intensive work-out he'd just been given by Tho and his men, the kicking around of the chair, and the struggles he'd put up, had stretched the cords binding his wrists together. He thought about this. It occurred to him that because they hadn't tied his feet to the chair legs, all he had to do was wriggle and shove a little, and he could be free of the chair. And after some slightly extravagant contortions he could—it was within the bounds of possibility—find himself standing up with his bound hands in front of him instead of behind. Which was a less negative position, certainly, than the one in which he was at present.

He thought about this some more. He could do it, he knew, except for the presence of the regular. In his hunched position he looked around the room. The chair he sat in was near the main table; that was a heavy piece of wood. It was solid. He knew that because Tho had heaved

144

it at him.

Maybe he could knock the guy over somehow—kick him in the balls, trip him up; anything—and so position it that the guy would fall back and hit his head against the table-edge.

Well, sure, it was an outside chance. *Anything* was an outside chance in his present position. Maybe he could fall on top of the guy's head with the chair, once he was down. Jesus, it was worth trying, and time was passing. It was right damn now or forget it. He raised his head.

'You speak English?' he said, as weakly as he could, though he really didn't have to try very hard.

The regular stared at him impassively.

Hardin nodded his head several times, wincing in not altogether counterfeit pain.

'The packet,' he mumbled. 'Had enough. The packet '

The regular stared at him some more.

'The packet,' croaked Hardin.

The regular glanced at the door then back at Hardin. He reached for his AK-47, then slowly walked across the room, the gun held in both hands pointing at Hardin. He touched Hardin's brow with the muzzle and Hardin gazed up at him, wide-eyed, then nodded to his left.

'There.'

The regular looked to his right, and the gun barrel shifted away from Hardin's head. Hardin thought that the positioning could not have been bettered if he'd actually asked the guy to place himself exactly where he was. His legs were apart, and the target was good. Hardin's right leg came up like a traffic signal, the boot connecting solidly with a meaty thud.

The regular's eyes bulged, his mouth gaped, and a tortured gasp erupted from his throat. He jack-knifed, dropping the rifle with a clatter on the bare boards, and lurched back, propelled by Hardin's other boot. He collapsed sideways on to the floor, still gasping, and his head missed the edge of the table by an inch or less. It was that close. He landed on his back.

Hardin gathered himself up to scramble crab-like in the chair towards him then stopped. He didn't understand what he was seeing.

145

The regular's body suddenly arched like a bow, his chest heaving upwards. His eyes squeezed tight shut and he made a sound like air escaping from a steam-engine valve. Blood appeared at the corners of his mouth. Dark blood, from somewhere deep inside. He flopped back down on to the boards and his eyes rolled upwards.

Hardin leaned forward, frowning, forgetting his pain in the effort to rationalise this development.

The door swung open, and another regular came in fast. He gazed at the sight, glanced back at the darkness outside, opened his mouth to yell then shut it again. He strode over to the other man's body, puzzlement mixed with anger on his face.

He bent down and turned the body over. Blood lay along the boards, and was smeared over the gap betwen, where the regular's back had rested. In between his shoulder blades was a rent in the cloth of his tunic, and a dark red oozing patch.

The second regular let the body roll back on to the floor and stood up. He began to harangue Hardin in Vietnamese. Hardin, his mind racing, tried hard to look as though he was listening. It was very difficult. Not because he could not understand Vietnamese—in fact he spoke it well—but because out of the corner of his eye he was seeing a thin rush mat behind the regular lift up and slide away from a portion of the floorboards—a trapdoor, in fact, out of which was emerging a man he'd never seen before in his life, a grunt, who was grinning like a madman, and holding what looked to be a wire garotte in his hands.

The grunt came up behind the Vietnamese silently and looped the wire over his head. An expression of shock flickered across the regular's face as he suddenly felt the kiss of the wire on his throat, to be replaced by horror as the wire tightened, then a devil's-mask rictus of stark agony as it sliced deep into his flesh and the jugular. Blood erupted from the sheared neck, drenching the front of his uniform, and then the head lolled, drooping loosely to one side.

The grunt let the body slump to the floor, unleashing the wire as he did so. He rubbed his fingers over the pants of his fatigues.

'A messy one,' he said. 'Least he didn't shit himself.'

146

He padded to the half-open door, glanced warily outside, then swung it closed. He slipped a knife from the belt of the man he'd just garotted and stooped beside Hardin, shearing through the cord that bound his wrists. He stood up, grinning again.

'You don't look so fucking good, Colonel,' he said.

III

Hardin stared down into the hole and said, 'You're Frank Marco, aren't you?'

Marco nodded, began to pull himself up into the room. He gently lowered the trap back into place. In his right hand he held a knife which was smeared red, and he began to clean it with a rag. Light glinted on the blade.

'Couldn't miss with this,' he said. 'You can see up into the room through the gaps in the boards an' he jus' fell right on top of me. Seemed a pity to waste a chance like that, Colonel Hardin.'

'You know who I am?'

Marco laughed sardonically.

'Jesus, do I know who you are! Listen, baby, you supposed to be dead. Alternatively, we—or some dudes we got with us—supposed to kill you if you still alive.'

'What the hell is that supposed to mean?'

'A long story is what that is supposed to mean, Colonel. Seems like someone gunnin' for you back in Nam. Someone really don't like you. Someone want you dead-dead-dead.'

'That,' said Hardin sourly, 'I know. So how do you fit in?'

Marco shrugged; sheathed the knife.

'Too long to tell, man. We were gonna get iced, too, but we could handle it. There's a bunch of survivors up on the hill, side of the ville. Jail-birds, like this dude here.' He indicated Garrett. 'Seems someone pulled 'em out the brig for M-16 fodder. The details escape me. All I know, we really ought to haul ass, before the slopes get back. All we got here is two AKs, an M-16, a knife, and a Goddamn garotte. Little enough, should the Yellow Peril come stormin' through the door.'

'The stuff in the cache, Captain,' said Garrett. He was sitting astride a chair and lighting a cigarette, seemingly oblivious of his surroundings.

'Cache?' said Hardin. 'You found the cache? How near is it?'

Marco pointed at the closed trap.

148

'Right damn there. We fell over it making like snakes under the hut. There's another trap immediately under this one, in the ground. Looks like a tunnel system, too. Climbed down and used a match. Couldn't see too well, but the cache itself looked like Fat City: rations, high-power R/T, grenades, MG an' tracer-belts in greased wraps. Like that.'

Hardin was pulling on his shirt. He had already cleaned himself up to a certain extent, with rags and some water from an earthenware pitcher and stuff from the medical-wrap, and was now starting to feel good. Adrenalin was pumping into him, toning up his system; he'd forgotten about the ache in his head, the bruises, the burns. The situation could still blow up—they could still all end up dead—but this breathing-space was just what he'd needed; he felt that the odds were beginning to fall in his favour.

Yet now that he could get out, now that a path had been cleared for him, he wasn't at all sure he wanted to leave. Just yet. What was uppermost in his mind was this courier. Who was he?

No, that was unimportant. *What* was he carrying? That, he felt, was the jackpot question. The *thieu tuong* was desperate to get his hands on it, and that meant bad news for somebody back in Nam; maybe bad news for a lot of people.

Hardin's loyalties were firm—however much he might buck the system, and whatever he might personally think of the conduct of the war. So he had to get hold of that packet. He was now the man on the spot, and his reactions must be governed by greater considerations than the simple need to escape and revenge himself upon Dempsey.

'Look, Colonel,' said Marco, 'it ain't that I'm chicken-hearted, or anything.' He paused. 'But.'

Hardin reached for his second gun-belt and was wrapping it round his waist when the door opened.

Garrett said 'Jesus!' and pushed himself backwards off the chair as though he'd just sat on a snake.

Framed in the doorway Tho stared at the scene for a split second. Behind him could be seen the two regulars, just reaching the top of the verandah steps and heaving a heavy generator between them. Hardin let go the gun-belt, snatched up the nearest AK and swung it round, even as Tho lunged sideways, disappearing from sight along the verandah. Hardin triggered off a burst, from left to right through the doorway, sending splotches of blood and shards of metal springing into the air as he caught the two men and the generator. The man on the left was punched out into the darkness and the one on the right sent into the verandah post and over, like an acrobat. Neither had time to scream.

Marco kicked the door shut then grabbed for another AK, flattening himself beside one of the windows.

'Kill the lights!' snapped Hardin.

In the gloom he could see Garrett at the window on the other side of the door, his head just above the sill as he peered through a crack in the hangings.

'Anything?'

'Uh-uh. Not a—Wait. Yeah, a movement. *Shit!* They're dowsing the fires in the square. That's gonna take the light-level down.'

Stooping, Marco moved back towards the trapdoor.

'So don't let's wait for the mothers. Let's split.'

'No!' Hardin's voice cut through the darkness like the crack of a whip. 'We hold.'

'You is shitting me, Colonel.'

'No shitting, Captain. We hold it here.'

'Jesus, they gonna blow our ass away!'

'Don't think they will. I think they'll try to capture us alive. Or at worst wounded. Whatever, we hold.'

'An' you bein' a colonel, that makes that an order, I guess.'

'Something like that.'

'Goddamn. When I get back to Base—*if* I get back to Base—I'm gonna see what my stars said for today. "Gloomy Monday, baby, stay put" is my hunch.'

Hardin ducked down and felt for the trap.

'You got sensitive fingers, Marco?'

'Dig it, Colonel. The chicks go wild 'bout the way I work.'

'So see how the MG and a box of grenades react.'

'Shee-it, Custer's Last Stand.'

Marco pushed his legs over the gap and swung down. Crouching beneath the building he could see between the

150

stone piles on which the hut had been erected, right across the central square. The two fires were still smouldering, but gave off little light. He sighed, and began to scrabble around in the dirt for the second trapdoor.

Above, Hardin joined Garrett at the window.

'Can you assemble an MG in the dark?'

'With my eyes closed.'

'Okay. Set it up facing the door. Give yourself plenty of room. Marco can handle the door. Don't fire till I tell you.'

Garrett shrugged.

'I was them, I'd just bring up a fucking mortar and blow our shit away.'

From below, Marco was sliding up bags and small boxes on to the floor of the room. Hardin padded over to the trap and hauled him up.

'I'm going down with an AK. From the right hand corner, behind one of the piles, I should have a clean sighting along the square at ground-level.'

'Now, you, uh . . . wouldn't be leavin' us to get nailed, now would you, Colonel?'

'C'mon, Captain. Get it together.'

Marco gave a nervous laugh.

'Listen, baby,' he said, 'I ought to be at the damn wheel of a damn gunship, that's where *I* ought to be. I ain't no fuckin' grunt. My old man, he was in Korea, 'long the Frozen Chosin. He said, get yourself some education, baby, don't be no fuckin' grunt. So I did, an' I ain't. Big fuckin' deal.' He helped Hardin through the trap. 'Watch your ass below. I left the ground-trap open. Swing to the left, or you'll go down the tube. Literally.'

Hardin landed on the ground and crouched down. He could feel a square of slatted wood in the dirt, and running his fingers along it he found a hinge fixed to a thicker structure, the lip of the hole that led down to the bunker below. As a cache, it was unusually placed; most caches were hidden in the jungle well away from a ville as a necessary precautionary measure. On the other hand, since this was a well-known fact, why not bury a cache below the headman's hut, where you least expected to find one? Maybe it was a smart move, after all.

He turned and wriggled across to the corner of the

151

building on his elbows, the AK-47 held in the crook of his arms. Peering round the corner pile he could see nothing that seemed suspicious as yet, but he was certain that it was only a matter of time before Tho sent his men out in a full-scale assault. It'd be useful to know how many EnVees there were, but useless wasting time speculating about it. Time was a commodity of which they'd been given short measure.

He could hear the faint click of steel on steel from above as Garrett assembled the MG, and hoped to hell Garrett's boast had not been an idle one, and, more important, that the greased wraps had been well-prepared by whoever had dropped the cache. It had seemed dry in the bunker, no smell of damp earth, but you could never tell.

The hell with it, he thought, some MGs jam for no damn reason at all. If it jams it jams. From the look of Garrett, he'd be the sort of guy who'd pick the damn thing up and go berserk. Might take out quite a few that way. He lined up across the square, and wished someone was positioned at the other corner. Nothing like cross-fire to damage a frontal rush.

He caught a sudden movement way over on the far left, then another: a flicker in deep shadow. He watched the spot intently, for several seconds, and was rewarded by more hurried shiftings in the darkness: three men in succession, at five-second intervals, leaping from one gap between the huts to the next. Now he could see similar activity on his right. They were massing for the attack.

He knew that the EnVees would be expecting resistance, and he figured that Tho meant to sacrifice a front line so that those behind would swamp the occupants of the hut in the final rush. You could only kill so many men in a bunch with a rifle—even an automatic rifle—before that bunch fell on top of you. What he hoped was that none of them would be prepared for the murderous fire of a tracered-up MG at point-blank range.

Suddenly the Vietnamese were no longer holding to the thicker shadows, but moving forward in short rushes away from the huts. From where he was, Hardin had a perfect line of fire, even through the steps—not a solid construction—but he held off, watching the EnVees getting closer, beginning to mass for the final charge up on to the verandah.

Now, he thought, as a group of men suddenly sprang into the lead and dashed forward, the others closing in behind them. The pad of their feet on the treads of the steps was a hurried, broken thudding, and he half-turned his head back towards the open trap and howled '*Now!*'

He heard the door crash open, broke out in a sweat of horror at the two-second silence, then grunted with relief as the MG opened up, an appalling, racketing clamour that split the heavy silence apart. All at once figures were crashing down on to the ground beside the steps to his left, staggering and crawling away from the blazing tracer-arcs he could see hurtling out across the plaza in long curving, brilliant lines. Then he heard the distinctive high-pitched stuttering crack of an AK-47, and knew that Marco was firing down at the verandah from one of the windows. Coolly, he sighted and began triggering off short bursts from his own AK into the groups of lurching figures, aiming low, going for the legs, sending them reeling and dancing and pitching over across the square like so many drunken marionettes.

Then they were running, scattering sideways, sprinting for the nearest cover in desperate, panic-stricken haste. And as the sound of the MG above broke off, Hardin was suddenly aware that rounds were beating the air all around him, and ricocheting off the stone-piles. It was as though he'd fallen into a wasp-nest: stone chips lashed his face and hands stingingly, and his ears were filled with the angry hum and whine of the ricochets.

Frantically he rolled for the trap, knowing that nothing could save him now but sheer speed. Under here, with rounds zipping every which way, it was as though the old joke had come true: he was a fish in a barrel.

Yet still he disciplined himself to heave the ground-trap shut and scuff dirt over the top of the boards before jumping up at the hole above and clawing his way over on to the floor of the hut.

Marco hauled him the final few inches.

'The mothers tagged you, huh?'

Hardin breathed out heavily; he felt it was a miracle he'd

only been scratched by flying stone-chips.

'You could say that.'

'You could say they got us all tagged now,' grunted Garrett. 'Only way out is through the fucking door, and I don't dig the idea of just walking out and seeing if your theory's a solid one.'

'Theory?'

'Yeah, that they don't wanna waste us, just wound us around a little.'

'Maybe.' Hardin turned to Marco. 'Where'd you put the grenades?'

Marco indicated a small box on the table.

'Okay, we're going to blow away the huts to our sides. Charlie's going to start sneaking round the backs of the huts and I want some fields of fire. Also it'll give us light. These hootches take a while to burn.'

Garrett squeezed himself down behind the 7.62 and Marco yanked open the door. Again the hut was filled with the ear-splitting thunder of the MG. Hardin ducked out to the right, pulling pins and tossing grenades, blinking in the sudden furious orange glare as the thatched-roof hut at right angles to the verandah split itself apart. He ducked back again, glancing up the verandah and seeing the next hut along already burning fiercely.

'I dunno, Colonel,' said Marco, 'seems to me like you dig the hot spots. You got a last-stand fixation. Shit, man, they not jus' gonna take all this shit lyin' down, you know?'

'They will. The honcho—the guy that was about to give me the ding-a-ling treatment—thinks I have something he wants. And the way I see it, Marco, he's just going to have to use the kid-glove treament, he wants it that bad.'

Marco was flat against the wall, craning his neck and peering out of his window. Light from the burning huts danced across his face.

'What I'm anxious to know is—what the fuck Olsen doing? That dude must think it's the end of the world down here.'

'He's got any sense,' said Garrett, 'he'll have faded out long since.'

154

IV

Olsen, staring down at the ville from the top of the knoll, was trying to figure out what exactly was happening. Like, who was who, for instance. It seemed to him that Marco and Garrett for certain must be in the headman's hut, but where had they found the MG that had created such a bloody shambles across the square?

On hearing the first sounds of the firefight, he'd pulled in Colby and the other two and gone to investigate. The entire action had been confusing because of the darkness, but even more confusing was the fact that after a lull the MG had suddenly opened up again and then two of the hootches had gone up, and it looked like the guys in the headman's hut had blown them.

'It's gotta be Marco in there,' said Doc Pepper. 'Gotta be, Sarge.'

'Yeah.'

'I mean, look, man, they blew the huts to give 'em light.'

'Could be, could be.'

Olsen's eyes drifted left to the bottom of the ville. Dark shapes scurried about in the gloom beyond the edges of the firelight's glow. He could make out no pattern of movement, but it was obvious the gooks weren't about to stay down there all night: they were working out how to hit the hut. It was weird that they didn't simply mortar it. Maybe they had no mortar; but if they hadn't, that was weird too.

The sharp stink of burning thatch filled his nostrils, blown by the night wind; sparks leapt high into the air, flaring; timber cracked and popped explosively.

He pointed across the valley.

'We could get a team across there, set up a fire-line,' he said musingly, 'then a team down at the bottom of this hillock and a team up near the headman's hut, to one side. Goddamn, Pepper, those fuckers wouldn't stand a chance!'

Doc Pepper sniggered.

'Will you listen to the man? Hey, Sarge, you only got eight men!'

'Less you, that's seven. Less Meeker and Stocker, that's five. Plus those two icers, that's seven. Plus me. We could still knock their shit out.'

'With no MG, mortar-team, Base fire-power. Hey, man! That's like—Wow! You clean this ville up, Sarge, and you could get to be a name in the books. You know, like whatsisname—the Kraut. Theory of attack. Clausewitz.'

Olsen gave a slow amused chuckle, a deep rumble from his chest. For the first time in a hog's age he was beginning to feel on top of a Goddamn situation. You had so much crap piled down on you, so many boots shoving you down in the mire, you tended to forget what that feeling was like. *Positive*. That's what he felt.

'Captain Marco's right, Pepper. You're a salty little shit. Now go get your Band-Aid pack together. We're going in.'

'Down there?' Doc Pepper stared at him, frankly incredulous. 'Against that crowd? Mother of Christ, man!'

Olsen braced himself, squaring his shoulders back. *Positive*.

'You gotta hack it, Pepper,' he said.

Down in the dip Olsen untied the two chopper gunners, pushed them to one side across the clearing.

'You two shitbirds,' he said, 'better get it together. You either join us or I leave you here, tied up. If I leave you here you either get found by Charlie and get yourselves screwed or you starve to death. You join us, you get your guns back. You could waste us, but I figure you'll figure it'd be frankly more sensible if you don't. You try and beat it you've still got a hell of a long walk to get back to Nam, and you could still get screwed by Charlie, and you could still starve your damn selves to death.'

Dondell rubbed his wrists, wincing.

'Sure, and we could just get our ass blown off down where the fighting is.'

'Right,' Olsen agreed, as though this hadn't occurred to him, 'you could frankly do that.' Then he leaned forward, smiling sourly. 'But if we make it out, at least you're on the winning side. I frankly don't know what the fuck is gonna happen to any of us if we get back to Nam, but could be if we pull this Hardin character out we may earn ourselves a pat on the back. Think about it.'

156

'Hardin's dead,' said Dondell. 'He got burned in the chopper crash.'

'Uh-uh. Hardin is alive and still very much kicking.'

'Shit,' grunted McGerr irritably. He sounded as though someone had just hung a bad speeding-ticket on him. 'Okay, I play ball. Never thought I'd be back running around in the crapping jungle again. I had a bellyful of that. Transferred to choppers *because* I didn't want to piss around down here no more.'

'Look where it got you,' said Olsen.

He turned, beckoned to Colby.

'I'm gonna put a team on you, Colby. I want some heavy fire laid down where I tell you, so you better not fuck me around.'

Colby had long since gotten over the traumas caused by Stocker. Back in the jungle again, he was beginning to feel on top. Hell, he'd had a whole year of this shit, he could handle it, and the feel of an M-16 in his hands had set him right up.

It was no good beating your brain apart with massive guilt-clubs about what happened way back when, because the truth was he couldn't remember anything about it. There was some nightmarish stuff slopping about right down there at the bottom of his mind, and on occasion it surfaced for a couple of seconds—like when someone just happened to mention to him in passing that he'd blown half his buddies away—but other than that very little that was concrete bothered him. He didn't try to understand this; just accepted it. It was the only thing you could do.

'Sure, Sarge. We gonna hit the ville? Gonna get some?'

'Yeah. You take O'Mara and Vogt, sit down at the bottom of the hill. The way I figure it the gooks are gonna be keeping to the other side of the square, it's an easier run for them. So you just pick 'em off as they run across. I'll be at the top end, their side, so if the MG opens up from the hut as well, the EnVees are gonna be crucified.'

Olsen tramped over to where Meeker was still lying on the ground. He reached down and took a handful of the man's fatigues, heaving him upwards.

'On your feet, Meeker. Up against a tree.'

He could see Meeker's face quite clearly in the fire-glow

from over the hill, and for the first time he saw a spark of intelligence flicker in the man's eyes. Meeker's brow wrinkled into a suspicious frown.

'You're going to leave me here?'

'Yeah.'

Actually, Olsen had no intention of doing that, not even when he'd threatened Dondell and McGerr. It was a measure for the moment; they could all be collected when the whole squad moved off later. *If* the squad, whole or otherwise, moved off later.

Meeker shook his head, suddenly smiling.

'No,' he said pleasantly, as though Olsen had just offered him a cigarette. 'You can't do that, Sergeant.'

Olsen gazed at him grimly.

'Wise up, son, that's exactly what I'm gonna do. Now move it.'

Meeker's face lost its smile.

'I said you cannot do that, Sergeant. I have my rights.'

Losing patience, Olsen began to hustle him towards one of the trees. Meeker drove his right fist into Olsen's stomach. It was a flea-bite, but it still stung. Olsen cuffed Meeker's face and Meeker began to scream and kick. Cursing, Olsen ducked back and hooked him on the chin. Meeker slumped to the ground.

'Vogt! Tie the sonuvabitch up and hitch yourself on to Colby when you're finished. And make it snappy—we haven't got all fucking night here!'

Leroy Vogt watched the others disappear up the hill and wondered if any other grunt in history had killed his sergeant a week after disembarkation, been thrown into the brig, been pulled out for a suicide mission, been threatened with death by his own countrymen, and had to tie up a guy, who'd been a lieutenant before he'd left his own men to be massacred, to a tree, watched by a madman, while the EnVees were mounting a vicious assault on a thatch-covered hootch not 200 yards away. God God *God*. You sure saw life in the US army.

He dragged Meeker face-down to the nearest tree, wrapped his arms round the trunk, and began to fumble with the rope.

'Vogt,' said Stocker.

He said it in a low, intense whisper that sent a frizz up Vogt's backbone. He glanced across the clearing. Stocker was still tied to his own tree; firmly, Vogt hoped.

'Vogt, I'm gonna do bad things to you. Very bad things.' There was unsuppressed malevolence in Stocker's voice. He was straining forward, his head thrust out at an unnatural angle and his face just caught by the faintly flickering light. 'I'm gonna nail you, Vogt. Nail you good. Been working at the ropes, Vogt. Can you jump quicker'n me, Vogt? Get to your gun before I do? You're gonna be a twisted fuckin' heap. Vogt. There's gonna be red all over your fuckin' lilywhite body.'

Vogt fumbled with the knots in the dark, hurriedly twisting length over length, tugging and pulling. It seemed tight. He couldn't see. It was dark round here; maybe Charlie had a fix on him. He kept glancing round as he fiddled with the cords.

'Gonna eat you up, Vogt,' came that blood-chilling crazy whisper, 'fuckin' suck your red blood.'

Vogt grabbed for his M-16 and scrambled up the hill. Even Charlie was preferable to this mad sonuvabith.

Stocker watched him go, chuckling. He saw Meeker's body twitch, one leg kick out convulsively. Meeker was coming to, and he was gonna do bad things to Meeker as well. That smart sackashit Olsen had forgotten to pick up Meeker's discarded Armalite, and he still had plenty of clips on him that no one had thought to take. All he had to do was get hold of that gun . . .

He shivered, fought down the rising tide of lust that was boiling up inside of him. Couldn't let go now. Gotta keep a tight hold on himself. Later, it would be all right to let the red flood of fury swamp him. But not now.

'Lieutenant!' he snapped. 'Quickly now! See if your ropes are loose. You might be able to get your hands together round the trunk.'

He watched, narrow-eyed, his breath coming in hardly controlled gasps, as Meeker pulled himself up round the tree. It all depended on whether Vogt had been too hasty in the dark, too shit-scared, too careless in his desire to get away. But Meeker seemed to have got the message; he was struggling with something. Jesus, if there was plenty of

159

slack and the trunk wasn't too thick...

Meeker staggered away from the tree like a zombie, rope still dangling from his right wrist, his left hand free.

'Damn, that was right smart, Lieutenant. Now me. But hurry! The damn gooks are comin' up the hill.'

Meeker stumbled across the clearing, rubbing his chin dazedly. He looked like a man who didn't know what planet he was on. Stocker, shivering with excitement, felt the man's hands pulling at his own knots, jerking at the ropes.

He tugged himself free at last and shook himself like a dog coming out of water. He couldn't feel his hands at all, and very soon his wrists were going to start hurting like hell as the circulation began to move again, and, and, and, and—and all that was blotted out as he lunged for the neatly stacked Armalite. He grabbed it and turned wildly towards Meeker who was standing near the tree, an expression of shock etched deep into his face.

Stocker moaned with pleasure. It felt like he was on fire. He sent half the mag slamming into Meeker, punching him over backwards. Meeker hit the tree and slithered down it, crumpling to the earth, leaving a sticky slime of blood down the bark. Stocker hobbled over to the twisted body and emptied the gun into it at point-blank range, opening it up, unzipping it, tearing it apart. Blood splashed and sprayed as the rounds tore into the bucking, jerking thing on the ground.

Stocker dropped the gun and fell to his knees, clutching at his groin, his body shuddering and quaking in paroxysms of shrill, squealing laughter.

V

Olsen didn't hear the chattering bursts of M-16 fire from the jungle clearing because, ten seconds before Stocker blew Lieutenant Meeker to shreds, he opened up himself.

It had been a perfect manoeuvre. He'd taken a risk, storming through the jungle at speed and not bothered too much about the noise-level in his haste to take his team right round behind the rear huts, and the risk had paid off. They'd bumped into no one. The gooks had all been pulled back to the bottom of the ville.

Now he and his men were spread out behind cover, looking down at the side of the ville, with the headman's hut to their left, just below the still burning hootch. There was plenty of room for the EnVees to sneak along past the hootches and, by the same token, plenty of room for Olsen and his men to mow them down.

Olsen chuckled quietly as he watched them sprinting in twos and threes along the pathway towards him. He let them come, let them build up into a solid wedge of figures below. It was a matter of gauging things just right, he thought, of knowing exactly the moment to strike—the moment that was maybe two or three seconds *before* they made their final rush. They'd be all keyed up, tense, ready to jump. You hit them at that precise psychological moment, and the shock alone was almost enough to destroy them.

He was projecting his own psyche out and into the minds of those little yellow men below. He knew what they were feeling because he'd been there himself, so many damn times before. With his stomach knotted up, his muscles tensed, his big frame quivering: like a horse before the gate went up.

And just as you're about to jump—*Bam*!

Just like now, he thought, squinting in the light from the fire. It's right. They're ready. *Now*!

At the sudden burst of firing, Marco, in the headman's hut, said, 'You were right, baby. Up the side way. Here they come!'—and then, 'Here they *don't* come. Hey, how is

161

it there's all this shootin', an' ain't nothin' hitting us?'

Hardin said, 'Up there—flashes. Someone's firing down from the jungle on to the path.'

'Fuckin' Olsen,' said Garrett. 'The sonuvabitch must have rocks in his head. I'd've lit out hours ago.'

'He's come to save my ass,' said Marco confidently. 'Where'd he be if I hadn't cut loose back at the LZ? Where'd you be, fuckhead, come to that? You an ungrateful mother, Garrett.'

As Marco was talking Hardin watched the flame-lit darkness intently. From this angle he couldn't see the results of the sudden action, only the muzzle-flashes from the treeline above. Whoever it was had caught the EnVees as they moved up towards the headman's hut. A smart piece of work. It would push the enemy through the huts and out on to the square, where Garrett could take them out completely with the MG.

He tugged at Marco's sleeve.

'Stay here. Nail anyone who looks like coming through. They may think we've split up, and there's only one of us in here. In which case they'll try storming the hut anyhow.'

He moved across the room, past the door, half-open with the MG poking through the gap, and peered round the other window. As he did so, he saw stabs of flame erupting from the side-alleys between the huts across the central plaza.

'Goddamn! There's someone to our left as well, firing directly across the square. This character has his head together.' He gestured to Garrett. 'Give 'em support. Straight down the middle.'

Spent shells clattered across the floor as Garrett opened up, sending tracer arcing fiercely through the night, and the Vietnamese were caught in interlocking fields of fire from three directions. M-16 fire from right and left ripped through the darkness, tearing into the fragile huts and out again the other side; tracer from the bucking MG hammered across the square in a controlled and murderous spray, kicking earth and rocks into the air, slicing through hut-struts and wooden railings. There was only one way the Vietnamese could go to escape that withering blast of destruction.

'*Hold!*' yelled Hardin, and the MG's shocking clamour ceased abruptly.

It was as though someone had thrown a switch and all sound had died. Hardin knew that the other two groups could not have heard him, and yet they'd stopped too, and all that could be heard was a thick silence, cloaking everything.

Hardin wriggled past the MG muzzle, through the gap in the door, and out on to the verandah. His eyes took in the scene, noting no movement whatsoever at the other end of the ville. He held his AK-47 tight to him, moving his body gently round from left to right.

'What was that guy's name?' he muttered back to Garrett. 'Olsen?'

'Check.'

'*Olsen!*'

More silence, then a movement to his right. He whipped round; relaxed. A tall, heavily-built GI was dropping down to the path beside the still-burning hootch.

* * *

'No one,' said Olsen. 'We've checked out in the huts, under the huts, behind the huts, all fucking round the huts, and there's no one. They've gone.'

'Cut out,' said Marco, lighting a cigarette. 'And good riddance, say I.'

'Not even any villagers.'

'Hah!' Marco blew smoke out through his nostrils. 'They split hours ago, you bet. But they'll be back.'

'So will the EnVees,' said Hardin.

They were standing to one side of the square, near one of the smouldering fires. Bodies lay around them, in twisted, unnatural attitudes, torn open by tracer, ripped by M-16 fire, in pools of slowly thickening blood. The stench of violent death mingled with the smell of burning thatch and wood, souring the night air.

'I've put Colby and Dondell at the edge of the ville, Colonel,' said Olsen, 'McGerr up back, and O'Mara and Garrett at each side. But not too far out. Frankly, sir, I gotta say we'd need about twenty damn men to keep this ville as

163

tight as I'd like it.'

'Which we don't have, Sergeant.'

'Nossir.'

Hardin stared at the nearest bodies.

'Any live ones, Sergeant?'

'Sir?'

'The EnVees. Were there any still alive?'

Olsen shrugged.

'Not after we'd finished, sir,' he said thinly. 'I figured, frankly, that we didn't need to clutter the place up and waste our damn medical resources, sir.'

Hardin nodded briefly; there could be no room for compassion when your own lives were on the line. In the jungle the law of the jungle obtained, pitiless as it was; uphold that law, and you survived.

Olsen coughed.

'With all respect, sir, is there any reason why we should be holding this ville? Seems to me, sir, frankly, we ought to be moving fast the other direction from the gooners.'

'There's a very good reason, Sergeant.'

Olsen nodded; shifted his body uncomfortably.

'Right, sir. What I figured I'd better pull Meeker and Stocker in . . .'

Hardin snapped round.

'Who did you say?'

'Meeker, sir. The guy that . . .'

'No—the other one. Did you say Stocker? Sergeant Alvin Stocker?'

'Well, I dunno about the Alvin, sir, but, yeah, he's a sergeant right enough. The guy that was gonna blow us away at the LZ. A mean motherfucker, sir, beggin' your pardon.'

Hardin laughed harshly. Everything was falling into place now. Stocker was Dempsey's creature—the guy who'd filled the Tun Phouc ditch up to the brim with bodies—and therefore Stocker *had* to be the courier.

'You've just bought our ticket out of here, Olsen. Where is he?'

'Got him tied up in the jungle, sir. Couldn't trust him or Meeker with guns.'

Adrenalin was pumping into Hardin's heart. Now at last

he could move. Plans tumbled through his mind as he stood there, staring at the flame-lit darkness around him. Attack the EnVees, grab their transport? Leave the EnVees alone and fade out quietly? All this would take time, and escape had to be fast. Very fast. That meant there was really only one way out now.

'There's an R/T in the cache under the hut, and there's a guy I know, Colonel Chuck Welland, who operates a special chopper raiding force out of Pen Kho, just across the border. If we can get through, they could be here in less than an hour.' He paused. 'If we can hold off the EnVees that long.'

'You figure they really will be back?' said Marco dubiously.

'I figure.'

Olsen yelled across the square.

'*Vogt*! Get your ass into the headman's hut and haul out the R/T.' He turned to Hardin. 'Vogt's our radio-man, sir. Might as well earn his keep.'

'A force of gunships,' said Hardin, 'and if anyone can do it, Welland can. He owes me.' He gestured at Marco. 'Bring me one of those guys who were all set to take you out on the LZ. I want to hear what he has to say before I talk to Stocker.'

Marco watched him walk towards the hut, a tall, erect, muscular figure carrying the AK-47 loosely in his right hand, a mag-belt slung across his back, grenades hanging in clusters from his fatigues, his gun-belt round his waist with the knife-sheath at the rear. One eye was still swollen and probably other aches and agonies were punching at his nervous system, but his stride was springy, bouncy, full of confidence.

'I'm gonna bring the guys in anyway,' said Olsen. 'Place 'em where we can see 'em. I figure we don't frankly need no early warning system now. We know the Goddamn gooks are gonna hit us.'

'Yeah,' said Marco. 'So let's hope the gunships get here before we is all deep-sixed.' He laughed thinly. 'Gunships! You ever thought, Sarge—we *all* gunships. *Human* gunships. We got more badass weaponry and infernal Goddamn machines hangin' from us than any other

165

licensed killers in history. Only we could flap our fuckin'
arms an' take off into the wild yonder, they wouldn't need
no chopper-gunships at all.'

VI

In the hut Hardin set fire to a cigarette and tugged smoke deep into his lungs. In one corner Vogt was still fiddling with the radio, but there seemed little point in trying again. Reception had been bad, the voice at the other end of all those miles had been faint, tinny, destroyed at times by long, crackling bursts of static.

'Forget it,' he said to Vogt.

Twice he'd sent his request, giving the rough co-ordinates of the ville. It was all he could do. The radio had clearly not fared as well as the MG; you had to take the rough with the smooth.

McGerr entered, followed by Marco. Hardin hitched himself on to one corner of the table and gazed at the man.

'Okay,' he said icily, 'so let's hear your side of the story.'

McGerr glanced nervously round the room, not meeting Hardin's eyes.

'About,' continued Hardin, 'how you had to kill these guys, and make sure I was dead.'

'Well, that was it, Colonel. I mean, in a nutshell. Stocker called us in—me and Dondell and a guy called Endean, and the pilot Clode. Told us what we had to do. Said it was an order from way up top, and we had to keep our mouths sewn. Clode got sick—either that or he got cold feet at the last minute—and we ended up with Captain Marco piloting the chopper. Stocker got really mad . . .'

'No, no, *no!* Stocker did *not* get mad! Stocker is not mad at all, never has been. You gotta have your damn foul lying mouth closed for you, McGerr.'

At the sound of that crazily irascible, resentment-choked voice, Hardin felt a chill run up his spine, as though an undeniably dead man had suddenly sat up in front of him, smiled, reached out and stroked his cheek. It was not mere fear, but a shock of sheer, unadulterated, heart-jolting horror; an emotion which had never touched him before in his life.

Then he heard the bang of an Armalite, felt a whip-lash in the air above his right shoulder, and saw the top part of

McGerr's head explode into a foggy shower of blood and brains. The thought raced through his mind that as a snapshot it was an almost incredible piece of markmanship, and then McGerr's body collapsed to the floor at his feet.

His eyes took in Marco gaping behind his back, his face twisted into an expression of dumb incredulity, and Vogt crouching white-faced at the radio in one corner. And even though he'd never heard Stocker's voice before, he knew it was a stone-cold certainty he'd just heard it now, and that the man himself was standing in the open trap behind him.

'Well,' said Stocker, a faintly aggrieved note in his voice, 'I didn't get no charge outta *that*. Meeker was much more fun. Still, plenty of time, girls.'

Hardin heard scuffling sounds behind him, but dared not look round. There was a dull thud as the trapdoor fell into place.

'Don't want no sneaky little fucker to get the same idea as me.'

Hardin's eyes darted from left to right, his brain reviewing the situation. Vogt's M-16 was too far away, leaning against a chair. Marco's M-16 was slung from his shoulder; no way could the black rip it off and use it in the split-second that was all Stocker needed to blow him apart. Olsen, outside, would have heard the shot and would be investigating by now, but if Stocker was smart he'd stay beside the trap, out of the line of fire from any of the windows.

His right leg was swinging free as he sat on the edge of the table, his left foot supporting him. It was starting to ache from the tension of keeping utterly still and the weight of his body. He was suddenly aware that he was standing on something, and, very slowly, he dropped his head just enough to see what it was.

Part of a belt. Jesus, it was the belt he'd been fixing on when Tho appeared. He'd dropped it to the floor and then, in the rush of events, had forgotten about it. The holster-flap was open and there was a .45 automatic down there, just begging to be used. But *how*? How to reach down there to yank it out without getting his kidneys sprayed across the room?

'Always get my man,' chuckled Stocker. 'They've been

tryin' to stop me doing my job since this damn operation started, but you gotta get up early to beat ole Stock. Shit,' his voice dropped to a gleeful whisper, 'that back of yours presents a fine target, Hardin. Real broad. Got a notion to carve the flag out on there, in bullets.'

'So you're Stocker,' said Hardin.

'Right. That's me.'

'The guy at the Tun Phouc ditch.'

Stocker giggled.

'So you heard about that? Dempsey didn't keep it as tight as he figured. Still, all the more reason to nail your ass, Hardin. Don't want that little episode to get to be common fucking property.'

Hardin's hands were touching the table on each side of him. Now he gripped the wood tightly, tensing himself. In his mind's eye he could see how the table was positioned, how it was lined up, and he knew what could be done. Whether he could do what he had in mind was another matter.

'Dempsey's not as smart as he thinks, Stocker.'

'He'll do.'

'He's sure as hell not to be trusted, either.'

'How so?'

Hardin laughed.

'You don't really think you're going to get out of this alive once you've delivered that packet, do you?'

The taunt drifted into silence. Hardin went on.

'I mean, you're a liability, Stocker. The Tun Phouc business is not even half-tight, it's as leaky as a Goddamn sieve—and you're the key figure. Apart from Dempsey. So you can bet your ass, Stocker, that Dempsey'd feel a keen sense of relief with you out of the way. Fact is, Stocker, you're a dead man. The EnVees are going to take delivery of that packet and then nail your hide to the nearest hootch. In double time, Stocker.'

'In double time, fuckhead, I'm gonna nail *you!*' Stocker spat out, his voice rising. 'Gonna rip your skin apart, Hardin, blow it right away. Don't need no shitting excuse. I'm gonna . . .'

Hardin heaved back with all the power he could muster, and the table shot away from him, smashing into

169

something unseen behind. But Hardin was already on the floor, scrabbling at the belt-holster, yanking out the automatic and squirming round with the speed of a disturbed rattler. He fired along the floor, two-handed, emptying the magazine.

Above the hammer-blow explosions of the gun he heard Stocker shriek wildly, and then Marco was hurtling past his prone body, his right-boot kicking out. There was a metallic crack and an M-16 clattered into view, skittering along the floorboards. Hardin lunged for it, swept it up and jumped to his feet as the door crashed open behind him.

'Jesus,' said Olsen, 'it's that sonuvabitch Stocker! How in hell did he get here? I just sent O'Mara to bring him and Meeker in.'

'Better call him back,' said Hardin. 'From what we just heard you won't find much left of Meeker.'

He strode across the room to where Marco was staring down at the still figure.

'Pretty shootin',' the black murmured, slightly awed. 'Dig it, Colonel, you took both his fuckin' knee-caps out!'

Stocker had fainted from the shock. He was twisted up against the wall, breathing harshly, tiny bubbles frothing and popping at the corners of his mouth. The knees of his fatigues were a mess, with blood-soaked rents in the canvas; white bone, shattered and chipped, poked through amongst the scarlet mush. Blood was flowing freely down his legs.

'You want him alive,' asked Olsen, raising his Armalite, 'or should I finish the fucker off, Colonel?'

Hardin shook his head.

'Get that corpsman I saw with you. We're taking him back. I want this bastard to sing.'

He bent over the crumpled figure, patting the pockets of his fatigues, then grunted with satisfaction as he felt a flat oblong shape under a breast flap. He slid his hand in; fished out an oilskin wrap.

There were papers inside, and Marco watched as Hardin flipped through them, his frown of concentration wiping itself away to be replaced by an instant of shock then tight-faced fury.

'Bad news from home?' queried Marco.

170

Hardin looked up, stared at the black for a moment as though seeing nothing and no one, then jerked his head, Marco followed him to the other side of the room.

'You know anything about "Ebb-Tide"?'

Marco winced in thought.

'Something, I dunno. A faint bell, baby, but it ringin' a long way away. Maybe I just heard the name.'

'That's about all you would have heard. Paris peace talks. As well as pulling troops out of Nam in stages, the normal way, we're making a goodwill gesture at the table in less than a month. As the negotiations open all troops, all categories, will be pulled out of the Nam-Laos border area, between the fourteenth and fifteenth parallels. Operation Ebb-Tide. As a propaganda exercise it's a doozy. The EnVees will have to make some kind of strong reciprocal gesture or lose a lot of face. On the other hand they could get a hell of a lot of speed out of bringing up a heavy concentration of troops and attacking the pull-out from the rear. It wouldn't matter a damn to them that they'd be accused of warmongering; they'd've made their political point by humiliating us. More fodder for the peaceniks back in the World.'

Marco nodded.

'Sure. But they don't know it gonna happen, so . . .'

Hardin's smile was as cold as permafrost. He tapped the papers.

'If they get hold of these they'll know. The entire withdrawal plan, item by item, detail by detail, movement by movement.'

'Je-sus Ker-eest! That's a sonuvabitch of a sell-out! Y'mean this dude Dempsey . . .?' Marco's voice trailed off.

'Right. I couldn't figure out what it was that would have brought an EnVee high-ranker out into the wilds of Laos to pick up a lousy little packet. Now I know. Once these copies were in their hands, the Tet Offensive'd look like old-time dance night at Arthur Murray's. There'd have been a Goddamn massacre.'

He broke off, turned. Coming through the door was the young black, O'Mara. He'd been running. Sweat on his thin face shone in the hut's light, and he looked as sick as a dead raccoon. He jerked a thumb over his shoulder.

171

'Meeker's been blown to shit! Jesus, looks like some animal tore him apart!'

'We know it,' said Olsen. 'Get a fucking grip on yourself, O'Mara.'

'It ain't all, Sarge. Out there,' he gulped for breath, 'out there. Sweet Jesus, there's about a million gooners headin' our way!'

VII

They were all inside the darkened hut now, but Hardin counted heads. Marco and Olsen, Garrett, Pepper the corpsman, Vogt, Colby and O'Mara, the chopper-gunner Dondell. And Stocker.

He'd sent Olsen and Garrett out to check O'Mara's report. O'Mara could have been spooked, jumpy after falling over Meeker's bullet-torn body. From talking to Vogt, Hardin had gathered that O'Mara had been in some grim scene in the brig; he was still nervy from it. But from Olsen and Garrett had come only confirmation: movement in the jungle to the north of the ville, movement along the river to the east. With luck the EnVees could not have penetrated to the west, and that was their way out— through the tunnel Marco had seen below the headman's hut.

'What do we do with Stocker?' said Marco. 'Pepper cleaned him up, but no way he gonna walk.'

'Leave him,' grunted Hardin. 'What I've got on me'll be enough. You go first, Captain.'

Marco dropped down through the trapdoor into the cache. There was no light down here—with the open trap and everything else in darkness light would only act as a beckoning beacon to the gooks—but he knew what to do. As each grunt dropped through he pushed them to one side, telling them to grab space and hold fast. Hardin came through last, swinging the trap over on top of him.

'Okay. Light.'

Marco lit two squat candles he'd found in the hut and Hardin gazed around him. The cache hiding-place had been worked on; it was as sophisticated an underground chamber as he'd seen. Usually these tunnels were merely holes in the earth, tubes for human worms to wriggle along to escape whoever or whatever was preying on them. This looked as though it had been constructed by professionals—probably Special Forces men. The roof was well shored up, braced by lengths of timber, and there were wooden walls. The cache itself filled most of the chamber: boxes and crates, cartons of tinned food, clothes, flashlights, dobie bags full of ammunition and explosives. It was an Aladdin's Cave.

Hardin picked out a flare-pistol and some cartridges.

'Each man take as many grenades as he can handle, and as many clips of ammunition. We go out through the tunnel to where it surfaces then head for the high ground overlooking the ville. We dig in, and wait for the choppers. Soon as they arrive I flare 'em, and we start hitting the EnVees in the ville to show the choppers they're not dropping into a trap. Sergeant, you put the men out when we surface. Find a good holding position.'

'I got the tunnel, sir.'

Hardin looked across the chamber.

Dondell, a flashlight in one hand, was tearing sacking away from a hole in the far wall. He shone the light through into the gap.

'Dry, sir. Wooden walls, good bracing, and slats along the floor. Easy!'

Dondell scrambled in on hands and knees, and began to move along the narrow tunnel. It went straight for several yards then curved left, out of the reach of the beam of his flash. He heard someone behind him, but could not turn to see who it was. He crawled on, breathing easily. The air was surprisingly cool and fresh. Jesus, he thought, this is some Goddamn passage: there must be ventilation shafts every two or three yards.

Then he paused, sniffing deeply. Now a gust of warm air hit him, and getting hotter. Weird. There was something wrong with the light of his flash at the bend, too—it was angry red. But that couldn't be his beam. Then it was as though a tide of fire swept around the bend, filling the tunnel, engulfing him. He shrieked and writhed as flame washed over and around him, searing the skin from his face, the clothes from his body, the flesh from his bones.

Hardin, behind, smelt the air and hacked back with his boots, wrenching his head round as he did so.

'Flame-thrower!'

He scrambled backwards madly, shoving at whoever was behind him with his feet, not heeding the splinters of wood from the floor-slats that drove into his knees. Then

174

he was out of the tunnel-mouth and rolling to the side, as flame bloomed outwards from the hole in a roar of sound, curling upwards towards the roof as it died.

'They had the fucking tunnel tagged!'

Through the chamber drifted the smell of burning wood and the sickly-sweet stench of roasting human flesh. Rounds popped and cracked in the tunnel from Dondell's blazing body.

'Up through the trap! Tunnel's on fire!'

Marco heaved the trapdoor open, banged his Armalite over the lip and sprayed rounds wildly in all directions. Then he pulled himself over, and shoved the second trap upwards. He bent down and hauled the first grunt up, pushing him higher into the headman's hut almost in one movement.

Hardin came through at last and heaved Marco after the others like a sack of coal, clambering frantically through himself.

'Far end of the hut!' he snapped. 'That cache is going to blow any moment!' Then, *'Not the fucking door!'*

But Colby, panic-stricken, had already jerked the door open. He was halfway through it when a spray of AK-47 rounds from the square lashed his body and punched him back into the room. His shrill scream stopped abruptly as bullets took him full in the throat, half-severing his head from his shoulders.

Garrett lunged for the MG, still sitting by the door, and nudged it forwards, squeezing tracer out into the night in long crazy bursts.

'Fuckin' gook fuckers!' he howled.

Hardin dived across the room, yelling.

'Flat on the floor!'

There was a thunder-clap of sound that felt like someone had come up behind each of them and smashed his palms against their ears, then orange fire boiled upwards in a gusher through and around the trapdoor. The hut heaved upwards at the end as though it had been kicked, and canted over. Chairs and chests and tables rolled and slid across the floor, and part of the roof flew off. Then the structure came down again, thunderously, shifting off its stone piles. The floor broke up, boards snapping and cracking across, tearing apart as though they were made of paper. Dust rose like a mushroom cloud, rolling outwards, choking and blinding those inside.

Hardin had been lifted off the floor by the massive explosion and hurled into the far wall. Now he dragged himself to his knees, thinking: At least those little fuckers down the tunnel must've got theirs; the blow back should've cleaned 'em right out to the other Goddamn end.

He started yelling names and was astonished to discover that they'd all survived the blast. Not exactly unscathed, but what the hell—you couldn't expect miracles when you were right on top of a Special Forces arms cache that had just blown itself to atoms. Blood was oozing from cuts to his heads and arms, his fatigues were torn and shredded, and he felt as though Joe Frazier had been using him as a punch-bag.

The hut was a shambles, and one end was burning fiercely, casting a garish light on the scene. It wouldn't take long for the flames to spread to this end. In the dancing, hellish light figures could be seen struggling to pull themselves out from under upended tables, smashed crates, other debris.

'We get out of here now. Make for the next hut down, past the one we grenaded. Olsen, you still got some grenades?'

'Check, Colonel.'

'We're going to blow a gap between us and them, Marco, fan your men out. Move it!'

He scrambled across the rubble and burst out of a jagged hole in the hut wall, firing as he ran. Marco came after him, moving outwards and shooting to the right. Garrett took far left position, using an M-16, and saw men tumbling over as he swept an arc of fire across his path.

Hardin and Olsen sprinted down the square, past Hardin's target. They hurled grenades into the next hut along, through the windows. The hut shook with the explosions, the dry thatch taking hold almost instantly. Men in solar topees came running out of the doorway, screaming, their clothes on fire. Hardin sent them cartwheeling over with bursts from his AK. The thunder of

176

automatic rifles ripped through the village.

Now the EnVees were firing back, and rounds burnt the air around Hardin's ears. He pinpointed the spot—a hut across the plaza—and yelled to Olsen. As one, their right hands went back then over—once, twice—and the hut burst apart in a tremendous wash of flame.

They turned and ducked low, racing for the hut from which covering fire was now erupting, and jumped through the doorway past Marco, who was crouched down lashing the square with short bursts.

Hardin leant against the wall, wiping the sweat from his face with both hands. He was breathing heavily and his heart was pumping so that he could actually feel it through his fatigues.

'Better get some idea of the ammunition position.'

'I already did, Colonel,' said Olsen.'It ain't, frankly, good. We didn't have time to grab as much as we could've done from the cache. We're really fucking low. Vogt's got three rounds and no spare clips. O'Mara got a half a clip. I'm down to five rounds. Like that.'

'Maybe we should hit the trees at the back?' said Garrett. 'All I have left is the fucking garotte. Or maybe you're expecting some really close work, Colonel.'

'If they had the tunnel tagged, they have us ringed. Must've got it from one of the villagers they maybe held on to. Whatever, we have to hold because of the choppers.' And as he said this he thought: If they come, if Chuck Welland got the message, if, if, if, He tossed his spare automatic to Garrett. 'Never did get to use this fucker. You can take a few out with it.'

Garrett, beside the hut's window, grinned sardonically.

'That's right civilised of you, Colonel. Handy, too. 'Cos here the basstuds come.'

By the light of the blazing huts Hardin could see the Vietnamese streaming across the square from all directions, not even bothering to hide themselves. He poked his AK through the window and fired a burst into the advancing crowd, knowing as he did so that the *thieu tuong*, Tho, had sent his men on a suicide dash. They were going to keep coming until the Americans' ammunition was finished, and then they were going to burst over the

177

hut like a tidal wave.

'Jesus,' said Vogt, his eyes white blobs in his smoke-blackened face, his voice high-pitched, 'they're not even firing back. Oh my God, they're just coming straight at us. They don't give a shit!'

Garrett was using the automatic and cursing. Marco dropped his M-16 and went for his own .45 only seconds before Hardin threw down the AK-47 and did likewise. Now the sound of firing was intermittent, and the yells of the advancing Vietnamese drowned it out almost totally. Men fell to the ground, writhing, but the crowd surged on over them like the sea.

The door bulged and creaked as they hit it; Marco was now slashing with his knife at faces and hands that filled the window. Garrett and Vogt heaved furniture across the door, but the pressure from outside was enormous —the door burst inwards, hurling the fragile barricade aside.

Hardin pulled out the flare-pistol and fired it at the doorway. The flare whooshed across the narrow space and exploded amongst the EnVees blindingly, and two men became their own funeral pyres—reeling figures swathed in flames but still pushed onwards by the immense pressure from behind.

Hardin thrust his knife into the nearest Vietnamese, tugged it out, and elbowed the choking figure aside, flames searing his arms. He slashed the blade round in a savage arc, shearing into grinning faces that exploded redly at him, hacking at necks and throats. He could smell the blood now, hot and tangy, and adrenalin was turning him into an insane automaton whose only programmed impulse was to carve and chop and cut and slash. Then the blade, in its wild carving flourishes, met bone and he couldn't pull it out. A Vietnamese reached for him, clutched at his throat; another hammered on his face with a knotted fist; someone was kicking at his legs, and he felt himself being dragged downwards.

Then he winced, dazzled by a fierce eruption of orange light. He heard, dimly a sound like the roaring of beasts, and then a mighty wind smote the hut, gusting hotly into its interior, burning the breath out his lungs. The

Vietnamese were shrieking wildly, gabbling out in frenzied panic, and the massive pressure on him disappeared.

'The choppers!' screamed Vogt. 'Napalmed the huts! The fuckin' gunships are here!'

* * *

Hardin stood beside the port door of the lead chopper gazing round at the shambles that had once been a Laotian village.

Bodies lay everywhere, singly and in jumbled heaps. The line of long-houses the other side of the gunship was a wall of fire, with flames leaping high into the angry darkness, and banners of smoke whipping and swirling and shredding to nothing across the central plaza. On the opposite side huts burned too, but here the devastation was incomplete: a couple of blackened and smoking ruins, a hut with its roof-thatch alight, another whose walls were mostly blown in, two with sagging roofs; others further down, waiting patiently to be destroyed. The air was filled with heat and the stink of oil and an acrid gut-churning mix of burning thatch and seared flesh.

Hardin felt drained, felt that the scene was somehow unreal, a dreamscape. He was seeing a nightmarish vision of an appalling hell: the hell that was reserved for men who lived by violence.

He turned wearily and looked into the chopper. Marco was sprawled out on the floor, gazing up at the chopper roof. Garrett, caked blood over his face, was slumped against the door-gunner's canvas seat, sucking at a cigarette. Olsen stared out blindly at the ville, his face registering no emotion whatsoever. O'Mara and Vogt were both huddled figures in the rear, with blackened faces and burned fatigues. Doc Pepper was sitting hunched over his bent knees, his head drooping down.

The neat, trim, clean figure of Chuck Welland moved into his line of vision. Welland brushed at his thick black moustache with a brown hand.

'C'mon, John. Let's get the fuck outta here before them gooners decide to come back.'

Hardin glanced towards the bottom of the village and

179

saw that dawn was destroying the darkness on the eastern horizon. He stepped up into the chopper and sank down to the floor.

EPILOGUE

The sun through the car windscreen was warm and Hardin was grateful for it. It relaxed him, laved his slow healing flesh but did not make him feel sleepy or take the tension out of him. That was good. He needed the tension.

Positioned as it was, the rear-view mirror gave a clear, uncomplicated view of the main doors of the hotel off Tu Do. Hardin lit a cigarette and slumped back in his seat, taking in the street and the hotel frontage, his mind drifting lazily.

Dempsey's chief aide Captain Vernon Alkine was singing like a choirboy, sweet and loud and pure. Clode, the original chopper pilot, had been found dead in his quarters, sleeping-pills overdose—but this was being looked into. Files were being pulled from cellar shelves, dusted off and gazed at with shock and outrage. Odd incidents, previously thought to be part of the arbitrary, inexplicable pattern of war, were now all too easy to understand. Certain political murders which had taken place over the past four or five years were being looked at in a new light. A prominent member of the South Vietnamese government had fled the country, and President Thieu had sacked at least a dozen more in a surprise shake-up. Even more heads, it was said, were to roll before the month was out. A hell of a lot of maggots had come crawling out from under a hell of a lot of upturned stones. And the funny part about it, thought Hardin, was that most of this had nothing at all to do with the border pull-out. Which had been cancelled.

Another funny thing was that the guy at the centre of it all, General Ronald Clarke Dempsey himself, had vanished. Hardin had hoped he would. It made things easier. Because the funniest joke of all was that Hardin, and only Hardin, knew where he was.

Dempsey, it appeared, had a number of bolt-holes in Saigon—more even than Hardin had known about—and these had been jumped on as soon as Alkine had been pulled in and had started talking. But not the hotel off Tu

181

Do, and that meant that Dempsey hadn't told Alkine everything.

Hardin himself hadn't mentioned it in his own lengthy debriefings; he'd held on to the knowledge tightly, not even hinting at it. There was something about that hotel; its faded opulence seemed to suit Dempsey's character in a strange kind of way. He might have wheeled and dealed and played with people's lives, but he was strictly a yesterday-man, when you got right down to it. The villains of today were altogether smoother operators, quieter, dispassionate. Put against them, Dempsey was just too uncool. Like his hotel.

In the rear-view mirror a stocky figure appeared at the top of the hotel steps and Hardin butted his cigarette and watched as it made its way down to the street, holding to the shadow of the doorway for a long time before scurrying across the narrow sidewalk to the car parked beside the hotel.

Hardin felt a jolt of adrenalin boost his system. In truth, he hadn't been one hundred per cent certain of the hotel—ninety-nine, yes, but not the hundred—and it was good to know that his week's stake-out had not been a complete waste of time.

He climbed out of the car and walked unhurriedly across the street, reaching the other vehicle just as the starter whirred. He glanced up and down, saw nothing, pulled a gun from his pocket and pushed the barrel through the driver's window at the young Vietnamese behind the wheel.

'Leave it. Just grip the wheel.'

The Vietnamese's eyes flickered in panic and his hands clamped themselves tightly round the top of the wheel. Hardin gestured at Dempsey, in the back.

'Get out the car.'

Dempsey didn't move. He was wearing wrap-round dark glasses and Hardin couldn't see his eyes. Nothing moved on the man's fleshy face.

'You don't move, I blow your stomach away.'

Dempsey breathed out heavily. He opened the door and clambered out on to the sidewalk, not saying a word. Hardin leaned forward and slammed the door shut. He

182

gestured at the driver with his gun, and the car rocketed away up the street, its tyres squealing. Hardin reached out, put a finger round the top of Dempsey's glasses and tweaked them off. They clattered on to the sidewalk. Dempsey's face suddenly creased up into a fat, avuncular smile.

'Jesus, Hardin, you're a fucking survivor. Goddamnit, you are.'

'We'll get this over quickly,' said Hardin. 'I've got better things to do than hang around a Saigon street killing you.'

'Don't be a crapping goon, Hardin. Why kill me? What the fuck is the point? You got out, didn't you? What the fuck more d'you want?'

'Your Goddamn hide.'

Dempsey chuckled. He seemed very much at ease.

'Look, you've made your point, blown away a lot of good deals, screwed up my career. What good's killing me going to do? Why d'you want the icing on the crapping cake?'

'You're incredible, General, you know that? Utterly Goddamn incredible. I'm going to enjoy blowing you all over the fucking city.'

Dempsey made an irritated gesture with his right hand. A ring on his index ringer caught the sunlight and flashed briefly.

'Don't be silly, Hardin,' he said, as though talking to a fractious child. 'Lemme ask you this: how are you fixed? You know me, Hardin, I'm not entirely without friends even now, or worldly crapping goods. You think you've destroyed all my assets? No crapping way. I can do you some good, put some heavy business your way, let you into one or two interesting deals.'

'Start praying, General.'

Dempsey went on as though Hardin had said nothing.

'You want to kill me because of the sell-out to the EnVees? Is that what this is all about? That disgusts you? Jesus, you're like a knight in fucking armour. There's no percentage in that, Hardin, believe me. I mean, this is a dirty war. Chi had me by the balls, and he was squeezing hard.'

'He was squeezing hard,' said Hardin flatly.

'Sure. Some guys had closed in on one of my operations. Drug deal. Laos. They'd caught on; they were pushing me hard. They had to be iced, but I couldn't do it through the normal channels. I figured Chi could do me the favour. Naturally, I was horrified when he presented the bill, but what could I do?' Dempsey's voice now had a whining quality about it, as though he was truly aggrieved, truly pissed off. 'But, like I said, it's a dirty war. So the EnVees would've cold-cooked our guys. Jesus, they're doing it all the fucking time. What's so crapping special about it?'

'You really don't understand, Dempsey. You really have no Goddamn idea. The reason you're going to die is because when I got out of the jungle I found a wire for me, about a cousin of mine—reporter on a Rochester paper. He'd been found in his bathroom with his wrists slashed. Open razor. Suicide.'

Dempsey looked up at him, his expression wary.

'So what? You're now blaming me for some guy's death back in the World? You're outta your mind.'

Hardin laughed.

'Not as much as my cousin must've been.' He pushed the barrel of the gun into Dempsey's stomach, hard. Dempsey gasped. 'Oh, you did it. No question. Or you had your spook contacts deal with it. It was a quick job, General. Too damn quick. They didn't research their subject too well. The guy had a horror of open razors, knives, unsheathed blades of any Goddamn kind. Since he was a kid. Didn't even use a safety. And it just so happened that I recall, at our last meeting, mentioning him to you. It's an open and shut case, you fat bastard. I know exactly the way your fucking mind works.'

Dempsey licked his lips.

'Drastic situations call for drastic measures, Hardin,' he said tightly. 'Hell, you know that.'

Hardin lifted the gun and placed it against the man's forehead.

'Cold, isn't it. Where you're going, General, they'll warm you up for fucking sure.'

For the first time fear darted across Dempsey's eyes, like summer lightning. Beads of sweat rolled down his forehead.

'For Chrissake, Hardin, I don't hold anything against *you*.'

'Where d'you want it?'

Dempsey suddenly swung round and began to run. He ran up the narrow sun-slashed street towards Tu Do, and Hardin watched him go, smiling. He raised the gun, fired it into the air. Birds clattered off nearby roof-tops; somewhere a whistle shrilled. Dempsey had almost reached Tu Do when the explosion went off.

It wasn't a big one. There was a heavy, ripping thud from somewhere up Tu Do Street to the right, and the crash of glass. Tyres squealed. The noon-day drowsy silence was rent apart by shouts and yells. Dempsey changed direction, swerving to the left, then lurched to a standstill, turned, began to sprint across the street.

Gunfire sounded, the harsh rattle of M-16s. Dempsey screamed shrilly. He was slammed into the back of a parked car as though by an invisible fist, rebounded, tried to cling on to the bodywork, slid to the ground.

Hardin, slipping the gun back into his pocket, walked fast up the narrow street and crossed Tu Do. He stared down at Dempsey's slumped body and Dempsey's dead eyes stared back. Blood was smeared in thick streaks down the car's paintwork and pumped out on to the tarmac from holes in Dempsey's back.

Three Arvin MPs jumped out of a jeep and hurried across. They began to jabber at Hardin, until he waved his ID at them.

'You boys are either going to be congratulated,' he said, 'or pissed on from a great height.'

'How is this?'

'You've just nailed the guy half the US forces in Vietnam are looking for.'

He walked away up the street with long, easy strides, and Marco detached himself from a shop doorway, joining him on the sidewalk. Ahead a car lay in ruins beside a shattered shopfront. People were milling around and talking at the tops of their voices.

'Dempsey should've remembered his own advice,' said Hardin, lighting a cigarette. 'Hope you didn't kill anybody.'

185

Marco shook his head.

'Uh-uh. Too small, baby. Anyways, I only kill people out in bandit country, nail 'em with a chopper. Although,' he went on, frowning, 'the way things are, maybe I ain't even gonna get to do that any more. They is treatin' me with kid-gloves back at Base. Don't know what the fuck to do with me, seems like.'

'Check,' nodded Hardin.

'An', the other guys, they got shoved in some special slammer or other, pendin', like they say, enquiries. It's a weird situation, man. I dunno what the fuck we gonna do.'

'I know a place,' said Hardin thoughtfully, 'where we can smoke a couple of pipes of opium, forget our problems.' He glanced at Marco. 'You, uh . . . dig?'

'Fuckin'-A,' said Marco.

Photoset, printed and bound in Great Britain by
REDWOOD BURN LIMITED, Trowbridge, Wiltshire